THE JUMPMASTER

By Howard R. Simpson

THE JUMPMASTER

HOWARD R. SIMPSON

PUBLISHED FOR THE CRIME CLUB BY
DOUBLEDAY & COMPANY, INC.
GARDEN CITY, NEW YORK
1984

All of the characters in this book
are fictitious, and any resemblance
to actual persons, living or dead,
with the exception of historical personnages,
is purely coincidental.

Library of Congress Cataloging in Publication Data

Simpson, Howard R., 1925–
The jumpmaster.

(Crime club)
I. Title. II. Series.
PS3569.I49J8   1984   813'.54
ISBN 0-385-19382-3
Library of Congress Catalog Card Number 83–20671

First Edition

To Alice Turner

THE JUMPMASTER

CHAPTER I

The first bright fingers of golden sun ran along the walls of the Corniche, slit the shadows on the narrow streets of Endoume and reflected from the golden statue of the Virgin high above the Church of Notre-Dame de la Garde. A stiff sea breeze had cleansed the air and pushed a few cream puff clouds off toward Roquevaire leaving a blue sky over the city. Marseille awakened slowly. The Vieux Port and the *quais* were quiet and empty. A few early risers stood at the zinc bars of the cafés, sipping their espresso and reading the morning papers. The usual gay banter of the Midi between barman and client was absent. It would come later when the sun had moved overhead and the first glasses of pastis were poured.

Inspector Roger Bastide of the Marseille police filled his cup with black coffee and walked out onto the balcony of his apartment. He leaned on the railing, his hazel eyes blinking at the harbor. Flights of pigeons glided in to take up positions on the Quai des Belges near the cruise boat landings, waiting for the tourists to arrive and the vendors to open their stands. A large white yacht flying a British ensign had dropped its mooring lines in front of the fifteenth-century Mairie, its engines purring like a contented kitten as it moved astern. Bastide yawned and scratched his chest. He was a man of medium height with broad shoulders. His dark hair, showing the first flecks of gray, was cropped short for the summer weather. His thick mustache needed trimming and he'd gone without shaving the previous morning. He sipped the strong coffee and closed his eyes, savoring the warmth of the sun. Bastide had a Mediterranean face with high cheekbones and a deeply cleft chin. His broken nose, a memento of a wartime brawl in Oran, gave him a tough, pugnacious look.

He had taken the weekend off. His first weekend in over a year. There was no season for murder but mid-August was usually quiet. His last case had been closed three days ago. Some fool of a vegetable wholesaler who'd stabbed his mother-in-law while she'd been preparing a *pistou* in the family kitchen. Now that the investigation was over and the report written, Bastide's only lasting memory of the affair was the strange odor: a blend of rich, garlicky *pistou* and the sweet smell of fresh blood. The thought of food reminded him that he hadn't eaten breakfast. He finished his coffee, retied the belt of his bathrobe and left the balcony, his espadrille-clad feet shuffling over the tiled floor toward the kitchen.

Bastide's bachelor apartment was spare but well decorated in the Provençal style. The white walls of the living room were hung with two oil paintings of Marseille by local artists, friends who met each noon at the Café le Péano on the Cours d'Estienne d'Orves to roll dice for drinks and argue politics with the Corsican patron. The canvases were bright with reds, yellows and blues. A low bookcase ran along one side of the room. It was stocked with new best sellers, a long row of *Serie Noire* detective stories and some untouched classics bound in leather. The dining-room table of thick, bleached wood was decorated with a copper tray of dried flowers and marked with faded circles left by damp wine bottles. The kitchen was well stocked and laid out for a working cook. A braided chain of garlic hung near the stove next to the spice shelf. Heavy cast-iron pots shared wall space with bright copper pans and a brace of Sabatier knives in a wooden rack were fixed to the wall over a stolid butcher's block.

He went to the kitchen window and watched the British yacht swing round till its bow was pointed toward the harbor mouth. A stubby Marseille ferry boat hooted a warning and swung ponderously under the yacht's counter, clearing it by several feet. Bastide smoothed his mustache and ran his finger over the scar it was supposed to hide. A young pimp had given him that on the Rue Lulli five months after he'd joined the police. They'd wanted to ask the *maquereaux* some simple questions about a girl found floating in the Bassin de la Joliette, but the pimp had run out of the bar into Bastide's arms. A classic *coup de tête* had caught Bastide unprepared. The police doctor who'd stitched his lip had given him a lecture on keeping his chin close to his chest in a street fight.

Bastide cut a baguette of bread, sliced the piece in half and began to butter it. He hadn't made plans for his three-day holiday but as he put the two *tartines* under the grill he knew it would start with a good, leisurely lunch at La Mère Pascal.

The Air-Inter flight arrived on time. The jet approached Marignane airport from the sea, glided over the red roofed houses of old Martigues, and touched down without a jolt. Donald McCallister peered out from his window seat as the aircraft taxied toward the terminal building. He felt good. He hadn't been back to Provence since the war. It wasn't fear that had kept him in England every August; it was more a desire to forget the past. Unlike many veterans of the Special Operations Executive, or SOE, the war for him had been a bad period, best forgotten.

McCallister's doctor had convinced him he should make the trip. He'd said it was nothing too serious but they both knew that McCallister's heart was faulty. The doctor, because of the tests and his experience; McCallister, because of the very personal signals that marked each day. The numbness and tight pain, the sudden nighttime thumping and perspiration. The tiredness that came like a lead weight after breakfast and stayed with him till the early afternoon. McCallister had seen it in the mirror. At sixty-five he had considered himself in good physical condition. One year later, the dark pouches under his eyes, the unhealthy skin color and the tendency of his hands to shake, even in repose, had changed his mind. His doctor had insisted he go to France as if the voyage was a medical treatment.

"You need a change," he'd said, glaring over his bifocals at McCallister. "The shop will get along without you. Go see your French friends and fill up with some of that vino. It'll do you good."

Two days later a strange thing had happened. He'd been invited to lunch by the son of a wartime friend. The younger man worked for MI6 and McCallister hadn't seen him for years. They'd had a pleasant enough meal in the quiet confines of a Knightsbridge club, reminiscing and chatting inconsequentially. With the port and cheese, McCallister's host had gotten down to business. He asked if McCallister would mind doing a bit of work for MI6 while he was in France. It really didn't amount to much, merely keeping his eyes and ears open and making an informal report when he returned. MI6 would cover his air fare and provide an expense allowance. He could hardly refuse. Besides, it made him feel needed again.

Joseph Campi fidgeted at the base of the escalator that brought the disembarking passengers to the baggage collection area. There was a soggy Bastos cigarette in the corner of his mouth and he rubbed his hands together impatiently squinting at the terminal clock. He was a short, fat man with a tanned, bald head and a paunch hanging over his belt. He took a few steps to a refuse cylinder, spit his cigarette butt into it and lit another cigarette. His watery, dark eyes watched an Algerian family straggle by dragging their luggage and boxes tied with twine. He grimaced. He was a farmer, a country man who didn't like crowds . . . or North Africans.

The terminal public-address system informed the passengers of the Air-Inter flight from Paris that their luggage could now be claimed. Campi kept his eye on the top of the escalator. He wondered if he'd recognize Mc-Callister. It had been a long time. Surely he had changed. They had all changed.

McCallister had been their jumpmaster. He'd trained them well. Taught them how to use a parachute in all kinds of weather. Pushed them out of the swaying basket suspended from a lumpy barrage balloon and cursed them from on high for their sloppy landings. Later, he'd stood by the door of the transport plane and cracked them each sharply on the shoulder as they launched themselves into the damp air over the patchwork landscape of the English Downs. They'd dropped out of the

bellies of clumsy bombers and endured doubtful landings in bucking Lysanders until their fear was replaced by
a cautious professionalism. Then it had been time for the
true test, the French soil coming up to meet them in the
still, cloud-covered night. They had done their job.
Later, McCallister had come to join them and there had
been the bad morning and the dead.

Joseph Campi frowned, his dark eyebrows converging
over his bulbous nose. He was still frowning when Donald McCallister appeared on the escalator. Campi recognized him immediately. The Englishman held himself
erect as if he were still on parade but he looked smaller.
Campi forced a smile and moved toward the escalator,
waving his stubby arms in greeting.

The stone facade of La Mère Pascal was just shabby
enough to discourage the tourist trade. One corner of
the red awning over the terrace tables had been shredded by the mistral and a battered gray cat sunned itself
on the sill of an open window. The original Mère Pascal
had gone to her grave in 1950, mourned by three generations of Marseille gourmets. Fortunately, her daughter
Dominique had taken her place at the ovens and after
several years of hard work had earned her own reputa-
tion as a fine cook. You couldn't find a better *bouillabaisse*
on the coast. Her *pieds et paquets* in their rich sauce and
her bountiful *aïoli* guaranteed a steady and appreciative
local clientele.

Roger Bastide stood at the bar and watched Dominique's husband, Georges, pour a thin stream of iced
water into his glass of pastis.

"Enough," Bastide cautioned, raising his hand.
"*Pardi!* You'll drown it."

Georges put down the water pitcher and lifted his own glass to Bastide. They sipped their drinks and Georges went back to work, pouring glasses of white wine for a group of fishermen in blue denim work clothes. Bastide picked up the morning paper and glanced at the front page. Unemployment had risen; a racing cyclist had fallen and fractured his skull; a young Danish camper had been raped by a gang of *voyous* at Bandol and the August 15 holiday would probably be the hottest on record.

He pushed the paper aside and smoothed his mustache, looking out the door at the sunlit street. Women were coming back from the open market, their shopping bags filled with vegetables and fresh fish wrapped in newspapers. Tanned young campers with beards and backpacks were clomping over the cobblestones, heads lifted to read the street signs on the ancient walls. Well-dressed businessmen from the Bourse hurried by on their way to lunch at the yacht club and the restaurant Chez Arnould.

Bastide sipped his pastis. Ten years ago a three-day holiday would have meant a frantic search for an attractive partner, a sortie from Marseille to some small hotel in the Var or the Lubéron, romantic walks through the *garrigue*, candlelit dinners and long bouts of lovemaking in deep-mattressed beds. Now, at forty, he took a more relaxed approach. His desire and need for women hadn't diminished. But he had learned the virtues of occasional solitude, the refreshing quality of silence.

He thought of the two women in his life: one out of reach, the other available and both highly desirable. He had known Mireille Perraud since their lycée days together. She had been the teenage love of his life. Then there had been a year at the University of Aix-en-Provence for him and she had gone on to Paris and the Sorbonne. After a year he had dropped out of the university and sought a job in Paris, to be near Mireille. He found Mireille engaged to a young naval officer and Bastide's romantic world came apart. Emotionally on the rebound, he walked into a recruiting center and told the surprised sergeant he wanted to volunteer for Algeria.

Mireille had reentered his life two years ago. Her husband was on the admiral's staff in Toulon. She'd invited him to dinner in their quarters. She had been friendly, informal and deliciously beautiful. Worse, he had found he liked her husband. After that he'd seen them at least once a month. Each time it was torture. Thinking of her he saw the large blue eyes, the thick tawny hair and the beautiful tanned legs. The last time they'd been together he'd invited them to lunch at the Cercle Sportif. When she came out of the dressing room to join them at the pool even the old regulars took their straw sun hats off their faces and sat up to watch her approach. Her black bikini looked as if it had been spray painted on her body. Their eyes had met before she handed her towel to her husband and sat down. She must know how much he wanted her. He hadn't picked up the telephone since nor had she called him.

Janine Bourdet was altogether different. Their meeting had been a pure accident. A reception at the Préfecture of Marseille and a soggy hors d'oeuvre had brought them together. Roger Bastide had been invited, along with a few other younger inspectors, to leaven the heavy mix of businessmen, consular corps representatives, educators and government officials there to meet the new *préfet de police*.

Bored and ill at ease in his new Dior necktie and old flannel suit, Bastide had finished his champagne and put his empty glass on the buffet. Turning hurriedly he'd walked into the open-faced caviar sandwich Janine had been holding in her hand. The fish eggs and butter had redesigned the pattern of his tie. Recoiling from the collision, Janine had spotted her silk dress with champagne. There had been a flurry of excuses, wiping and dabbing. In atonement, Bastide had refilled Janine's champagne glass and requested one for himself. It was only after he'd handed her the glass and they'd edged away from the buffet that he noticed how attractive she was.

Bastide shook the ice cubes in his pastis. He frowned, remembering that first night. After fifteen minutes of conversation he felt he'd known her a long time. She wasn't what you would call beautiful. Her mouth was too large, her hips a bit wide beneath a slender waist; the dark eyes set too far apart and the black hair too short for his taste. But somehow, together, the amalgam worked. She radiated a natural sexuality, a *chienne* that had fascinated him.

They'd exchanged abbreviated biographies over the hum and rattle of the reception. He had never met a woman as direct as Janine Bourdet. Her frankness had left him openmouthed. He'd covered his embarrassment with a quick gulp of champagne. Janine had been a call girl. She'd told him this, looking directly into his eyes, waiting to gauge his reaction. Bastide had thought it a joke. She'd quickly set him straight.

"It's simple enough," she'd said. "You're a *poulet*. I was a *poule*."

Instinctively, he'd glanced around to see if they'd been overheard. She'd laughed.

"Oh," she whispered, leaning toward him, "don't worry. I belong here. I'm a fixture at these affairs. I'm now the 'friend' of Monsieur Théobald Gautier. The *préfet* insisted I come even though Théo is off in Geneva counting his money. Are you as bored here as I am?"

They'd left discreetly to have dinner together at La Mère Pascal. Between mouthfuls Janine had clarified her relationship with Gautier. She'd been his mistress for six years. With the death of his wife she'd become his companion. His money, his status and his advanced age made the arrangement palatable to the realistic, mercantile society of Marseille. Janine, formerly a scarlet woman, had now taken on an inoffensive shade of pink.

When they'd finished dinner Bastide had invited her to his apartment for cognac and coffee. Dazed by his good luck he'd led her up the old stone stairway to his apartment and rushed to the kitchen while she looked out on the Vieux Port from the balcony. They'd had their cognac and he'd forgotten the coffee, leaving it to bubble into a thick syrup. They'd talked of themselves and he'd been surprised to find himself matching her confidences with his own. They laughed often. She'd been particularly exciting when she laughed, her long-lashed, almond eyes almost closed, her even white teeth showing. At one point, his hand came to rest on her thigh. He hadn't moved it and they had both stopped laughing. Sensing his mood she had slipped into the bedroom telling him to turn off the lamp, so the apartment was lit only by the reflected lights of the cafés and the neons along the Vieux Port.

She had come to him wearing only her high heels and a

thin golden chain around her waist, the unsteady light playing over her full, large-nippled breasts. She'd been practiced, direct and genuinely sensual. Her lovemaking had been an explosive, physical gift, a revelation that had begun in the shadows of the living room and left him perspiring on his rumpled bed. He'd seen her often since then. Thinking of her made him smile with pleasure.

"*Alors,* Roger! You sleeping?" Dominique's raucous voice shook him out of his reverie. She'd come out of the kitchen and behind the bar to pour herself a glass of iced rosé.

"Madame," Bastide replied with exaggerated formality. "I am thinking."

"Ha!" she snorted. "A *flic* who thinks. It's a miracle."

Dominique was a handsome woman, all generous curves and cascading black hair, small gold earrings and a humorous mouth. She raised one brown arm and emptied half her glass. There were beads of perspiration on her forehead. "*Oh là là!*" she said, shaking her head. "It's hot." She filled Bastide's glass and topped it with water. "Not working?" she asked, wiping her hands on a bar towel.

"No. I am resting." He lifted his glass in a silent toast to her.

"You're eating with us today?"

"Yes. What do you recommend?"

"The sardines. So fresh they are winking at me. Grilled and filled with my spinach stuffing. Do they temp you?"

"They do."

"I would offer you some tender slices of lamb but I must save it for tomorrow."

"Tomorrow?"

"Yes, the fifteenth of August. The day of the 1944

landings. We have a big luncheon. The veterans will be coming down from the ceremony at Fort Saint-Nicolas hungry and thirsty. I cannot disappoint them."

"How many?" Bastide asked.

"Thirty, all hung with medals and dragging their flags along." She sighed. "Do men never tire of playing soldier?"

Bastide remembered his Army days. "No," he replied, "I'm afraid they don't."

"Well," Dominique said, washing her glass and turning toward the kitchen, "go find a table. I'll grill your sardines."

Bastide took his half-finished glass of pastis to a table by the window and sat down. He had forgotten the landing anniversary. He calculated a moment. Thirty-eight years ago on August 15 the Allies had landed in Southern France. Tomorrow there would be wreath-laying ceremonies and speeches at the beach memorials behind the coast and in the hills where airborne troops liberated the small villages in the early hours of the attack. There would also be clannish ceremonies of the various Resistance groups commemorating the comrades who didn't live to see the liberation.

Jean, an elderly waiter with sore feet, brought Bastide a basket of fresh bread and a bottle of white wine from the Bodin vineyard in Cassis. As he sipped the crisp, dry wine, Bastide thought how lucky he was not to have planned a trip on the clogged autoroutes over the holiday period.

When the sizzling sardines reached his table he was reflecting how wise he had been not to have joined a veteran's organization. If he had, he'd have been rising early the next morning to stand in the sun listening to the vacuous speeches of tired old men and ambitious young politicians.

The Valley of Roucas lies to the northeast of Marseille among a high ridge of rocky hills and spare forests of pine and scrub oak. In the early morning hours of August 15 the air was still. A mist hung like fog over the valley floor. A thin spring moon moved slowly across the sky like a luminous splinter. A nervous gray hare hopped along the sand track of the winding mountain road, darted through the pickets of a low fence and hid behind a square marble tombstone, its nose twitching as it sniffed the air for the odor of danger.

There were only five tombstones in the small, well-kept cemetery. The hare, reassured that no immediate danger threatened, left some moist droppings on the grass and bounded across the enclosure to disappear into the sage.

By 10 A.M. the mist had disappeared, grasshoppers were springing out of the dry brush and the cicadas had taken up their buzzing and clicking in the oaks. The sound of engines in low gear reached the valley from the north ridge. A slow moving convoy of cars wound down the dirt road, leaving a pall of yellow dust behind them.

The lead car, a black Peugeot with an Army license plate, pulled to a stop beside the cemetery. The driver jumped out to open the door for two officers. They dusted off their uniforms, squared their kepis and turned to watch the arrival of the others. The driver opened the trunk of the Peugeot and carefully removed a wreath of blue, white and red flowers.

The second car was from the Préfecture in Marseille. It deposited a young, lower-ranking official, who shook hands solemnly with the officers before ordering his driver to turn his car around facing the departure route. Other car doors slammed as their passengers exchanged greetings and unloaded flag staffs and more wreaths. Most of the men were elderly or middle-aged. They wore dark suits hung with brightly colored medals that clinked together as they walked to the cemetery. Some of them had berets pulled forward over their brows. Others used canes and walked with difficulty. There was one woman among them. A petite, gray-haired woman in a tailored suit who wore the twisted barbed wire emblem of the wartime concentration camps on her lapel.

Joseph Campi's car was the last to park. He swung his wheel violently, backing dangerously close to the thick trunk of an old pine and slamming down the brake pedal.

"Eh bah, merde!" he grumbled, pushing open his door. "Those idiots should have parked further on. They didn't leave any room for us."

Donald McCallister got out of Campi's small car with difficulty. He straightened his back and smiled.

"Joseph, you haven't changed. Always impatient. Always angry." He laughed and walked around the car to join Campi.

McCallister wore a dark pin-striped suit, his Special Forces Club tie and a black bowler. The decorations and campaign medals on his chest glinted as they stepped from the shade into the searing sunlight.

McCallister smoothed the wisps of thin gray hair above his ears and wished he hadn't helped Campi finish that last bottle of wine the night before. His head throbbed and his eyesight was a bit fuzzy around the edges. He would have liked to have felt better this morning. It was going to be the most difficult part of his visit, meeting surviving members of the Réseau Renard after all the years that had passed. Remembering each of them, fumbling for words to say about those who had died and, worst of all, hoping no one would bring up the events of that morning thirty-eight years ago that had made the small, isolated cemetery necessary.

"Mr. McCallister?" an obviously British voice called to him. He turned to see a sandy-haired young man with spectacles coming toward him.

"Yes," he replied, slightly puzzled, accepting the man's soft, outstretched hand.

"I'm from the British Consulate. Peter Hampton, vice consul. We always send someone here on the fifteenth. I'm honored to meet you, sir. Pleased that you could come."

"Oh," McCallister replied, "thank you." He paused, saw Campi frowning at them and introduced him to the British vice consul. They walked together into the cemetery enclosure exchanging pleasantries.

"*Bon sang!*" someone shouted loudly, producing a disapproving glance from one of the officers. "It's the major!" It was Raoul Senac, big, bluff and gauche as ever. He rushed forward, grabbed McCallister in a bear hug and kissed him wetly on both cheeks. His affectionate assault almost toppled McCallister but he regained his balance and pumped Senac's hand, laughingly keeping him at a distance to avoid further kisses.

"You old bandit! How are you?" McCallister asked, watching Senac's bloodshot eyes for a clue to his true feelings and finding only friendship and unfeigned joy.

"Come, greet the *commandant!*" Senac called to the other veterans and they shuffled over, some grinning hesitantly, to shake McCallister's hand. He felt a weight lifted from him as he greeted each of them: Colbert, the little radio operator with the mournful expression, now wrinkled and more mournful than ever; Duverger, the weapons expert. Were those cataracts in his eyes? Blanchard, a thin stick of a man who ate more than all of them and was always hungry. He looked like a yellowed straw that a gust of wind would break in two. And finally Hugo Paradisi, who came forward from behind the group, his once luxuriant hair carefully combed to cover a bald spot, and shook hands quickly, without warmth. McCallister thought he saw what he had dreaded. Paradisi's eyes had held his for only a few seconds but it had been enough. They were black and burning, full of hate.

McCallister felt slightly ill. He noticed the weight of his bowler and the heat of the sun. Senac grabbed his arm and led him closer to the graves.

"*Commandant,* do you remember the cognac we liberated from the Fritz?" he said loudly. "How you could drink that cognac!"

The official from the Préfecture sidled close to them and made a shushing sound. "Remember the dead," he said pontifically, nodding toward the headstones.

Senac peered at him in surprise. "Little man," he said slowly, tapping the rhythm of his words with his forefinger on the official's lapel, "these are *our* dead. They know us. They don't know you."

The British vice consul smiled nervously. McCallister pulled Senac away from the official, calming him. "*Ça va, ça va,*" he told him, "it's about to begin."

They formed themselves into two straggling lines, the beribboned tricolors sagging over the graves at different angles. An Army chaplain stepped forward and began the service. McCallister stood with his bowler in one hand and looked up at the ridgeline on the other side of the valley. It hadn't changed. It had been up there, among the jagged rocks and the wild thyme, that it had happened. It had been the killing ground.

Notice of the airdrop had come in a code that only he could decipher. When he'd finished he'd read the message twice and rechecked his cipher booklet to make sure he hadn't made a mistake. It was to be a special drop. The contents would be packed in arms canisters. Three canisters would be dropped. Two would contain ammunition boxes. The third, marked with red tape, would hold some weapons parts they had requested. The boxes were not to be opened nor were any French members of his team to assist in retrieving them. He and Sergeant Whipple were to bury the two boxes at a map coordinate easily identified by a small stone shrine. The third canister would be carried back to the bivouac. Headquarters underlined that the successful completion of this simple mission took priority over any other contingency. The message made it clear that his responsibility ended when the boxes were buried. Luckily, the French members of the réseau had been too tired by the climb to argue when McCallister had told them he and the sergeant would handle the drop that night.

The Dakota appeared at 2 A.M. over a DZ one mile from their camp. It was weaving and dipping like a fat gull, the pilot trying to cut drop time to a minimum and return to the Mediterranean without coming within range of the German antiaircraft batteries at Toulon and Marseille. They'd heard the crack of the chutes, watched them blossom against the stars and drop slowly downward, the shrouds pulled taut by their loads. Two canisters had thudded into the brush intact but the third had torched and crashed into the rocks. When they'd reached it McCallister had stopped cold. On the ground at the base of the rocks there had been a bright sheen with a trace of moonlight. He'd crouched down and flicked on his hooded signal torch. The smashed canister and the splintered wooden ammunition box had dumped a shimmering torrent of gold coins over the sandy soil. He'd picked one up, held it close to the thin beam of light and recognized the fine tracery of laurel leaves and the profile of Louis Napoleon etched into the gold. Luckily, most of the heavy paper container rolls hadn't cracked open.

They'd buried the chutes on the spot and dragged the one unbroken and unmarked canister over five hundred yards of rough terrain to the shrine, panting and pausing to rest while the perspiration stung their eyes and dropped off their noses. They had worked without speaking, the sergeant wielding his entrenching tool as quietly as possible.

The first pink light was pushing up over the mountain ridges when they'd finished. McCallister had made a quick decision. They didn't have time before dawn to gather the scattered coins and bury them at the shrine. He and the sergeant went back to the drop zone to shovel sand over the gold and camouflage the spot with branches of juniper and spiky gorse. They returned to the bivouac carrying the container with the weapons parts between them. Senac had been brewing coffee over a smokeless fire. Paradisi, who had taken the last night watch, had just turned in under the shade of a granite outcropping.

The chaplain finished and stepped aside. He was very young. McCallister wondered if the words he had spoken had any real meaning to him. He supposed they didn't. What a farce. Now the representative of the Préfecture cleared his throat. He had some notes in his hand and he glanced at them before speaking.

"Thirty-eight years ago," he began, "a group of brave men . . ."

McCallister scanned the rank of veterans across from him. There were some there he didn't know. Probably the SOE agents who'd worked in the towns and cities, feeding information to London and sending messages about German movements and plans out to him. One man shifted the flagstaff he was holding to the crook of his left arm and he blew his nose noisily into a handkerchief. The gray-haired woman had put on dark glasses. She stood with her head bowed while one of her thin hands toyed nervously with the pleat of her skirt. Who was she? Very likely sent off to the camps before he'd ever come to France. He felt uncomfortable and thirsty. His pin-striped suit was much too heavy for this weather. When one of the officers began to talk McCallister's eyes lifted once more to the ridgeline.

They had come out of the sun, fast and so low McCallister had seen the faces of the pilots and the first man of the stick standing in the cargo door. Three troop-carrying Junkers with dun camouflage and white-etched black crosses on their fuselage. The parachutists came out like acrobats, one after the other, arms spread as if high diving. The surprised members of the Réseau Renard had lost precious seconds watching them tumble earthward. McCallister remembered thinking that no British jumpmaster would allow such a short, dangerous drop. One chute, caught in an airpocket between peaks, did torch and the German's body smashed into the ground, raising a cloud of dust.

Then there had been shouting and firing with McCallister trying to bring order out of confusion. The billowing chutes seemed directly over them but most of them fell away from the ridge and landed on the west slope. He remembered Senac, his old MAS rifle steadied on a rock, calmly aiming and firing at the descending parachutists. Sergeant Whipple had been laying down fire with his

Sten and Blanchard had been busy seeing that everyone had a supply of grenades.

The Junkers had banked and come back to drop another stick. This time the lumbering aircraft raked their position with machine-gun fire. They were forced to keep their heads down and seek shelter among the rocks. Most of the Germans in the second stick had managed to reach the ground untouched. They had been good, probably specially selected. They moved quickly up the rough slope, taking advantage of cover, their camouflaged parachute jackets making them hard to spot. The ripping fire of a Spandau machine gun was soon chipping chunks of granite off the rock above McCallister's head. He had known some of his men were hit but he hadn't known who.

"Mon Dieu, mon Dieu!" someone had sobbed nearby. He had crawled toward the sound to find a young man who had just joined them lying on his back, the top of his right shoulder gone, the white bone of his clavicle exposed. Bright arterial blood was sluicing out of his wound with every heartbeat. McCallister had tried to stop the flow with slippery, shaking hands but the blood had slowed and stopped as the boy died.

There had been the hollow cough of the mortar then. The first ranging shot was over but the second dropped among them, its fragments spanging from rock to rock.

Sergeant Whipple had caught one. It had entered his right eye and exited under his left ear. After that it had been too difficult to keep track of casualties. The parachutists were working their way closer. McCallister had remembered the urgency of the message from headquarters. He realized he must make a decision. He had rolled onto his back and put his field glasses on the distant shrine, then shifted them to the approximate area of the scattered gold. If he could slip off the ridge, make his way back to the cache and remain hidden till the Germans left, he could still bury the coins. A dark blur tumbled through his field of vision and exploded with a yellow flash. He put down his binoculars and a second potato-masher grenade arced over the ridge.

"Kamerad!" *someone had shouted.* "Ne tirez pas!" *He couldn't recognize the voice but he knew it was one of his men. He'd slipped from the rocks and rolled down an incline hidden from the advancing Germans. Once into the brush he had stumbled further down the hill, zigzagging his way to the cache. For a moment he had thought he'd lost it but the branches they had broken for camouflage before dawn were already dried, showing light against the dark of the live foliage.*

Panting, on his knees, he had been about to hide in a thick growth of gorse when a rock from up the slope bounded past him. Revolver in hand he'd turned to face the threat. Someone was coming toward him but the sun had been in his eyes. That was the last thing he remembered of that day.

The high-velocity bullet hit him seconds before the crack of the rifle echoed through the valley. The force of the impact threw him forward between the headstones. His bowler rolled on its brim till it was stopped by one of the wreaths. In the moment of shocked silence that followed, the British vice consul thought McCallister's skull resembled a badly opened Stilton. Then he walked to a nearby tree and threw up.

CHAPTER II

Barnabé "Babar" Mattei had the weekend duty. He'd driven along the Quai du Port in his battered green Mercedes, up the hill past the Cathedral, crowded with Assumption Day worshipers, and parked in Inspector Bastide's slot at the Hôtel de Police. There was no real need for him to sit in the office on August 15. He only had to be on call. But Mattei had six noisy children and he preferred to have his wife cope with them on a holiday. He sat in Bastide's office tapping on a typewriter with two fingers, trying to complete a report that was already one week late. Mattei was a handsome Corsican with a weight problem. He considered himself attractive to women and took great care with his appearance. His wavy black hair was razor cut and trimmed at one of the best shops in Marseille. His opulent sideburns grew down his cheeks. His olive skin glowed from a liberal application of expensive after-shave lotion. He was dressed in a light-blue sport shirt and gray cotton slacks. His blazer was draped over his chair. He wore a holstered Colt .38-caliber police special.

Mattei was rarely aware of his increased girth. He was a powerful man, solidly muscled under the fat. He could move quickly when he had to. The only time he ever seriously considered a diet was before, during and after his annual physical examination. He would fret for a few days prior to the examination, wondering what new horror the scales would reveal. He would be depressed the day he knew. The worst always followed. He could count on being summoned to the office of Commissaire Aynard, a dour, thin Lyonnais, who would invariably lecture him on his weight, threaten temporary suspension pending proof that Mattei was shedding kilos and send him on his way suggesting a lunch of carrot salad and Vichy water. Mattei had found the best antidote to this ordeal was to hurry to the Jambon de Parme restaurant for a lunch of tortellini washed down with Valpolicella.

The lilt of a martial "Marseillaise" drifted in through the open window. The ceremonies at the Fort Saint-Nicolas were coming to a close. The Foreign Legion band from Aubagne were playing. He had seen them unloading instruments from their trucks as he'd driven to the Hôtel de Police. He cursed and banged the typewriter with his fist. The *t* was sticking and his report looked as if it was being written by someone with a stutter.

Bastide's office was functional and ugly. The Hôtel de Police was an ancient building and most of the offices had high ceilings and wasted space. Bastide's battered wooden desk faced the smudged windows. Mattei's desk was in a far corner. Both Bastide and Mattei sat with their backs to an inner wall. Three fluorescent tubes suspended from the ceiling threw a greenish light over the filing cabinets, the exhibition case with its grisly mementos of past cases and a cluttered board covered with mug shots, official notes, duty rosters and alert notices from the Ministry of the Interior, the Direction de la Surveillance du Territoire—or DST—and Interpol. Mattei had reserved the lower right-hand corner of the board for a rotating exhibit of nude and seminude females that he assiduously clipped each month from the raunchiest French periodicals.

The bells of the Cathedral chimed and the pigeons preening on the facade of the Hôtel de Police fluttered into the air. Mattei glanced at his watch and frowned. It was already noon and he still hadn't finished. Of course, he reasoned, it could wait till tomorrow. He stood up, drew the dusty plastic cover over the typewriter and carried it to a nearby table. He'd stop at the Bar de la Marine for a pastis and get home in time for another before lunch. He must remember to tell the switchboard where he'd be. He pulled his blazer over his sport shirt, adjusted his wide belt and headed for the door. He had gone down one flight of the dirty, concrete stairway when he heard the phone ringing behind him. Cursing, he turned and climbed the stairs two at a time.

"*Allo?*" The voice was hesitant, uncertain and very faint.

"*Allo! Allo!*" Mattei shouted. "Inspector Mattei here."

"*Allo?* Police Judiciare?"

"Yes, who is it?"

"*Allo?* I'd like the Police Judiciare."

Mattei rolled his eyes in frustration. "*Mince alors!* You've got the Police Judiciare. Homicide. What is it you want?"

"This is the Gendarmerie at Gémenos. Sous-Brigadier Fauchet speaking."

"Very well, Fauchet," Mattei replied with controlled patience.

"We have a . . ." The line buzzed with interference. ". . . to talk with you."

"What?" Mattei shouted. "I didn't hear you. What is it?"

An excited, youthful voice came on the line. "How soon can you come?"

Mattei was losing his calm. A vein stood out on his forehead and he cursed quietly to himself. "Come where? Is this a comedy? Who are you?"

"Sous-Préfet Bardot . . . ah . . . from Marseille. There's been a murder here."

"Where?"

"At the Resistance cemetery at Roucas . . . during the ceremony. An Englishman . . . shot."

Mattei was taking notes in a broad, sprawling script.

"I've called the Préfecture. They gave me your number. The gendarmes are waiting for you. Can you come quickly?"

"Very well. We'll be there as soon as we can. When did they find the body?"

"Ah, we didn't find it. It . . . he was with us. He died with us. Beside us."

"How was he killed?"

"Probably with a rifle . . . at long range."

"*Monsieur le sous-préfet*, can I have your name once again?"

"Bardot, Jacques Bardot."

"We'll be there."

Mattei put down the telephone. The bells were still clanging outside, the pigeons wheeling around the square. He dialed Bastide's number. He let the telephone ring till he was sure Bastide was out. Then he clicked the receiver till the police operator came on the line. He asked for the contact number Bastide had left with the switchboard and dialed it.

"Péano!"

He recognized the hoarse voice of the bar's patron. "Is Bastide there?"

"*C'est vous,* Mattei?"

"Yes," he muttered, irritated by such an easy identification.

"A moment." He could hear the patron shouting through a din of loud talk, laughter and clattering dishes.

"*Salut,* Babar!" Bastide sounded in high spirits. "How goes it?"

"Not well," he told his boss glumly. "More cold meat on our hands."

"Well, I'm sure you can handle it. Another family quarrel, a teenage gang fight or a *règlement de compte?*"

Mattei cleared his throat. "None of those. A foreigner. An Englishman. Shot during a ceremony this morning at Roucas. The Prefecture's involved. The Gendarmerie is involved. I'm sorry, but I think we'll need you on this one."

"*Bonne mère!*" Bastide groaned, his holiday slipping away from him.

"I'll be at the Péano in fifteen minutes," Mattei told him.

"No, pick me up in front of my place. I've got to change."

"All right."

"Are the gendarmes sealing the escape routes?"

"I didn't ask."

"Well . . . ask!"

"On August fifteenth? With all the traffic?"

"They must try."

"Very well."

"Oh . . . and get the office sedan out of the garage. I won't risk traveling in that German revenge you drive."

Mattei chuckled. "As you wish, *patron,*" he replied, ringing off.

After calling the Gendarmerie, Mattei rang the forensic lab and asked the technician on duty to alert Dr. Colona.

McCallister's body lay exactly as it had fallen. The gendarmes had covered his shattered head with a plastic sheet. Most of the veterans were sitting in the shade, talking in low voices while two gendarmes moved among them asking questions and taking notes. An officious gendarme with highly polished boots was guarding the corpse, his hands clasped behind him. Senac sat on a nearby headstone staring at the ground. Blanchard was beside him, one thin hand on Senac's shoulder.

"He came all this way," Senac said, shaking his head. "It is unthinkable. Who could have done this thing?"

Blanchard glanced over his shoulder at the far ridge but said nothing. Joseph Campi walked up to them, wreathed in cigarette smoke. His tanned pate glistened with sweat. *"Alors,* Raoul?" he addressed Senac. "No need to sit here all day. You can't help him now. Have you two spoken with the gendarmes?"

Blanchard nodded.

"Well, they know how to reach us," Campi said. "Let's go into town. We need a drink." Senac got up slowly and the three men walked toward their car. Other veterans gathered up their flags and followed. They were in the middle of the dusty road when they saw a black Citroën sedan careening toward them. It braked to a quick stop throwing a cloud of light dust over their dark suits. Bastide and Mattei climbed out and walked to the group.

"Messieurs," Mattei nodded a greeting. "You're not leaving?" He stopped to wait for an answer as Bastide walked on to the cemetery, gesturing for the senior gendarme to join him.

Campi spoke for the group. "We are finished with the police," he told Mattei. "They have our testimony and addresses."

Mattei smiled and wagged his right forefinger back and forth. "I regret, gentlemen, but you have not spoken to the police yet. You see, *we* are the police."

It had become known as the "Battle of McCallister's Ridge" among the members of the SOE inquiry board that opened the investigation in London late in 1945. But the battle interested them only in so much as it touched on the disappearance of the gold. The inquiry had lasted three years. A long succession of witnesses had been called in to be questioned, but progress was blocked where McCallister's testimony had left it, on a sunbaked hill in Provence. Search teams, investigations and interrogations had produced nothing. They'd even watched McCallister carefully, putting a tail on him for endless months, hoping he'd suddenly nip off to Bermuda or the Riviera to throw money around and drink champagne. They were disappointed. His big spending had consisted of three pints and a Highland malt in his local on Saturday night.

The surviving members of the Réseau Renard were questioned in a roundabout manner by experts posing as postaction interviewers interested only in the German attack and possible internal betrayal. They were sure that

the ground they covered and the questions they asked
would have revealed any hidden knowledge of the gold
drop or its disposition. They had drawn a blank. An
effort was made to trace the officers and men of the
German parachute unit who had participated in the operation. It failed. Wehrmacht records showed the survivors had been killed to a man, trying to block the Soviet
advance on the Elbe. The file now sat on a shelf in a
storage center for classified documents eighty miles
north of London. A brief notation of its title, subject
matter and location was listed among thousands of
others in a rarely used booklet locked in a safe at MI6
headquarters in Century House, Westminster. An even
more important file had been transferred to the Foreign
Office where it slept among others judged too sensitive
for the storage center. It was stamped MOST SECRET and
titled "Operation Red Gold." It had been minuted the
previous year by a thorough, high-ranking assistant to
the Foreign Secretary who believed in vetting classified
documents on an annual basis to see what could be de-
classified or destroyed. His minute on Operation Red
Gold was brief and to the point. "Still highly sensitive,"
he'd written. "Maintain current restricted access."

   The overloaded bus wheezed around the last corner
and entered the town of La Ciotat. The passengers were
hot and uncomfortable from their trip down from Saint-
Maximin but the freshening wind from the sea revived
them. A group of young vacationers were singing a Gilbert Bécaud song but they didn't know all the words. The
older passengers were fanning themselves and eating
fresh apricots purchased at a roadside stand. The bus
pulled to a jerking stop near the center of town, its ex-

haust spewing black smoke, waves of heat rising over the hood. The disembarking passengers struggled through the aisle with their parcels and baggage. The driver took a smudged handkerchief from his pocket and wiped the gritty dust from his damp forehead.

A small man with a springy step was the third to get off. He wore a white cotton cap, a white sport shirt, baggy blue shorts and leather sandals. He carried a blue plastic *filet* holding two shiny *boules* and a long canvas bag that appeared to be quite heavy. His eyes were hidden by dark glasses. His arms were deeply tanned and sinewy. There was a tattoo in blue ink on his right forearm: an anchor entwined by a coiled rope with the word COMMANDO under it.

He walked along the cracked pavement to the street corner and turned left toward the beach. Within ten minutes he had reached the Hôtel Rose Thé. The beach in front of the hotel was packed with people, the water dotted with swimmers. Small sailboats darted dangerously among the bathers. As he turned into the hotel's garden, he could smell the odor of grilled steak and fried potatoes from the beachside restaurants.

One of the employees, a young girl, called to him from the desk. "Ah, Monsieur Brannec! And the *boules?* Did you win?"

"Eh, non, ma petite," he replied in a voice like grating sandpaper. "But almost."

She handed him his key with its heavy numbered brass plaque. "You missed your lunch."

"It is of no importance," he replied, hefting his canvas bag higher before climbing the stairs. "Time for my siesta."

Once in the room he tossed the bag onto the wide bed,

dropped his *boules* in a corner, locked the door and pushed the night bolt. He unzipped the bag and removed a long package wrapped in a soft piece of chamois. He undid the wrapping carefully. The rifle was a masterpiece. He ran his fingers over its burnished stock. Not many like it in circulation. It had been specially made for the GIGN, the French antiterrorist unit, by Mannlicher. Even the metal seemed to have a special, exclusive texture. He detached the telescopic sight, put it on a bedside table, rewrapped the rifle and zipped it back into the bag. He put the bag in the armoire behind his suitcase. Taking off his dark glasses he picked up the sight and walked to the window. Standing back in the shadow, he put his blue eyes to the sight and brought it to bear on the beach. The delicate zoom control worked like that of an expensive camera. It was as if he were on the beach. He panned slowly from left to right and stopped to focus on a bikini-clad mother standing with her hands on her hips watching her two small children at the water's edge. Her behind was beautifully molded, like a perfect peach.

"Formidable," he murmured quietly to himself. *"Quelle fesse!"* He walked to the armoire, opened his suitcase, took out a metal box and put the sight in its bed of foam-rubber padding. What a pity, he thought. By midnight the rifle and the sight would be at the bottom of the sea. It didn't seem right. But those were his instructions and he always followed orders.

Inspector Roger Bastide was concentrating on his cooking. The chicken was ready for stuffing, the chopped onions were simmering in butter on the bottom of the thick casserole and the figs were peeled and sliced. The kitchen was hot despite the open window and he wiped his forehead with a small towel he'd wrapped around his neck. Barnabé Mattei appeared in the kitchen door. He handed the inspector a glass of pastis. Mattei had taken off his coat and loosened the knot of his tie. He put his own glass on the kitchen table and rolled up his shirt sleeves.

Bastide gulped his drink, his eye on the onions. When they turned translucent he added a handful of chopped chicken gizzard and liver to the casserole and followed them with the fresh figs.

"I don't know how you do it," Mattei mused, watching his boss. "I can't cook an egg. Not that I want to."

Bastide grunted in reply. As the gizzards and liver sautéed he added the rice, stirring it around in the butter till each grain shone. "Your problem, Babar," Bastide commented, "is that you don't appreciate what skill and care goes into cooking. You'd eat anything put before you."

Mattei shrugged and patted his belly. "That may be true. But I'm not a savage, you know. I appreciate good food."

Bastide added a minimum of water to the mixture, ground a pepper mill over it, threw in four pinches of salt and turned the heat high to bring everything to a boil. He checked his oven to make sure it was heating properly. Mattei reached for Bastide's pastis glass and left the room to replenish it. Bastide turned down the heat and wiped his hands. It would take twenty-five minutes to simmer. He followed Mattei into the living room. Mattei had his glass ready. There was an unspoken rule in Bastide's apartment that business was not discussed in the kitchen. Now, as they walked out onto the terrace, Mattei made his delayed report.

"I saw Dr. Colona when he'd finished. Not much we didn't know ourselves. But the angle of the projectile fascinated him."

Bastide shrugged and pushed his open left hand upward. "Colona's not paid to be fascinated," he said.

"He was puzzled about the firing point. The ridge is very far away, a long range for such a small target."

Bastide frowned. "He knows it came from the ridge? I don't. From the state of the Englishman's head I don't see how he can be sure."

"Oh, Colona did a lot of measuring. Talked about projectile force and brain throw."

Bastide grimaced. "So what was Colona's conclusion? He always goes beyond his medical prerogatives."

Mattei chuckled. "He told me to tell you he thinks it was a military sniper's rifle."

"Remarkable deduction," Bastide growled. "Why doesn't that old fool stick to his butcher knives and his dissecting table?"

Mattei was silent. "Go on," Bastide told him. "What else?"

"No luck with roadblocks. We searched the ridge and I had a team combing the woods and the paths. Not a thing. The sand isn't deep up there. Mostly rocks and stone chips; no chance of footprints. We scoured each parapet and cranny hoping to find the rifleman's position or an empty cartridge casing. Nothing."

Bastide rubbed his chin and watched a fishing trawler chug slowly toward the quai. The traffic below was thick with cars returning from the Plage de Prado. "And the witnesses," he said thoughtfully, "the veterans. The Réseau Renard. It was a Socialist group, wasn't it?"

"Yes. Some of them have changed colors since the war

but in 1944 they were mostly Socialists. Our people did some quick research. The Renard had contacts with the Francs-Tireurs Partisans—Beaulieu's group—operating in the Toulon region and with Colonel Lebrun and his right-wing companions in the Var. But the British called the shots from London. They controlled the purse strings and the supply."

"Ah," Bastide sighed, *"les anglais.* They are a puzzle to me."

"I don't like them," Mattei said, finishing his pastis with a flourish. "My older brother was at Mers-el-Kebir. Saw the whole fleet sunk by British shells. His description was terrible. A slaughterhouse. They are a cold people."

"I think we will have trouble with this one," Bastide said ruefully.

"Why?"

"Too much of it is under the surface. Commissaire Aynard had a call from the Ministry today. They asked for a daily report on our progress. An exceptional request."

Mattei glanced toward the pastis bottle on the living room table but decided he'd had enough. He shook his head. "A cold people," he repeated. "That vice consul is a little tit sucker. I don't like him. When they took the body, he insisted that every bone chip be gathered up and put in plastic bags. He was rude to one of our technicians."

Bastide laughed. *"Pardi!* Babar is becoming sensitive."

"No, not at all. I just don't like the English. Look, *patron,* I must get home or my wife will grill my balls."

"My regards to her. You must both come to dinner soon."

"With pleasure. *Allez*, till tomorrow."

Bastide heard the door slam as Mattei left. The sun was weakening. A brisk wind was blowing over the harbor, rippling the water and tugging at the bright clusters of balloons held by the vendors along the Quai des Belges. He looked at his watch. It was time to check the oven.

The kitchen was redolent with the simmering stuffing. It was ready. All the liquid had disappeared and the rice was perfect. He spooned the mixture into the cavity of the chicken till it was full and closed the gap with two metal skewers. He poured some olive oil over the chicken's skin, salted it and added a dash of cayenne pepper. He lifted the chicken onto a lightly oiled baking pan and pushed it into the hot oven. Forty-five minutes should do it. They would be able to eat at eight-thirty. There was no rush. Janine was always late.

By the time she arrived Bastide had prepared a chicory salad and the chicken was brown and crisp. Janine brought an armful of sunflowers and a bottle of Gigondas. The wind had died, so they moved the table onto the terrace and ate by candlelight. A new gold chain glinted on Janine's tanned chest. Bastide paused in his carving and raised an eyebrow, pointing to the necklace with his knife.

"New?"

"Yes. You like it?"

He shrugged and lifted a piece of breast meat onto her plate.

"Théo found it among his family's heirlooms. Eighteen-karat gold and quite heavy."

Bastide put a steaming mound of fig-and-rice dressing beside the chicken and handed Janine her plate.

"Hmmm," she sighed, closing her eyes. "Ambrosia."

He said nothing, serving himself. She took her first forkful, her eyes on Bastide, one strand of dark hair across her forehead. She smiled. "Roger, you're not jealous of dear Théo?"

"Not at all." He lifted his glass of wine.

Janine threw back her head and laughed. She put down her fork, picked up her chair and moved around the table beside Bastide, pulling her place mat and plate along. "Now," she said, her hand on the inside of his thigh, "I can touch you in the right place. You know, Roger, no one pleases me as you do."

The blackboard was almost covered with notations, names, arrows and numbers. Babar Mattei watched Inspector Bastide write the name of Colonel Lebrun and add a question mark. Bastide had taken off his necktie. They had been working for hours trying to draw bits and pieces of information together. They still hadn't achieved any coherence. One of Bastide's men, a young detective who had cut himself shaving that morning, cleared his throat and asked a question.

"Are we sure it has to do with the war? The Englishman might have had other enemies . . . outside of France."

"That's unlikely," Bastide replied, writing "Jean Beaulieu, FTP," under the colonel's name and adding another question mark.

"Perhaps the bullet was meant for someone else?" the young man persisted.

Mattei glanced at him. "Have you been smoking in the narcotics section?" he asked. "A stray bullet doesn't make a perfect hit like that. It was too professional."

"It's still possible."

"True. It's also possible that I like little boys, but the odds are against it."

Bastide put the chalk down and stepped back from the board. "Now, let's go over it once more. The Englishman was in command. He had chosen the bivouac on the ridge where they were attacked. When it became desperate, he deserted his men . . . or so Paradisi claims. The others don't deny it. They only say he was not there when they surrendered."

"So," Mattei sighed, "they hated him."

Bastide nodded slowly. "At least some of them did."

"But, damn it," Mattei continued, "they were all at the cemetery."

"You're right. There are no other survivors. But it doesn't have to be one of the *réseau.* It could have been an accomplice or a hired assassin."

"And the other groups? Beaulieu and his *cocos* or the colonel and his military types."

"We're going to have to talk to them. None of them liked each other. Luckily for France they hated the Germans a bit more."

"But someone pulled the trigger," the young detective said, touching the minute razor cuts on his neck.

Mattei turned to him slowly. "I don't know what we'd do without you, Pierre," he said sarcastically. "We old ones need fresh insights like yours."

The telephone rang and Bastide answered it.

"Yes, yes, right away." He put it down and reached for his necktie. "It's the *commissaire,*" he told them. "I'll be back in a minute." He knotted his tie, pulled it tight and put on his light cotton jacket. Once out in the hall, he climbed the stairs to Aynard's floor, passing two detectives of the Narcotics Squad.

"*Salut,* Bastide!" a sandy-haired detective wearing jeans and a three-day beard greeted him. "How's the stiff trade?"

"Very well, thank you," Bastide replied. "I see you're still dressing like a juvenile delinquent."

"Undercover work, you know. Quite demanding."

"*Merde!*" Bastide commented over his shoulder.

Commissaire Aynard was waiting and told him to enter on the first knock. He pointed a thin finger at a chair in front of his desk and Bastide sat down. Aynard had the air of a Calvinist minister. A badly cut blue suit bunched up on his shoulders and the white cuffs of his shirt reached almost to his knuckles. His rimless spectacles were far down his nose. "*Mon cher* Bastide," he began.

Bastide was forewarned. It would be a long lecture.

". . . I am not sure you and your people realize the ramifications of the McCallister murder. I thought it best if I explained things more thoroughly. You must be extremely careful . . ."

Bastide listened with half an ear as the commissaire droned on. Aynard had been his superior almost a year now. A difficult year. Aynard had been sent from Lyon to tidy up the Marseille police after a scandal involving the in-house beating of a North African suspect. Aynard had seen his assignment as an opportunity to impose his conservative order on the Marseillais and teach them how a police organization was supposed to operate. For him, it was like an assignment to the colonies. He'd found his task very difficult. The meridional character was beyond his comprehension. At times he was certain an organized vendetta of noncooperation had been directed against him. The frustrations of his work and the demands of his social-climbing wife had aggravated his dormant ulcer. The drawer of his desk was full of antacid tablets.

". . . there are political aspects that you may not have considered," Aynard continued. "I want you to keep me better informed. As you know, you can call me at any time, night or day."

Bastide nodded and was about to speak but Aynard raised his hand, stopping him. "You've got to watch your men. Keep them on a short leash. Particularly Mattei. I've had reports about him throwing his weight around. He might be able to get away with that in Corsica but not here . . . on the mainland. Now, for instance, what is on your schedule for today?"

"We're reviewing all the information we have right now. Later, I plan to question the two other regional Resistance groups that the Réseau Renard had contact with during the war."

Commissaire Aynard frowned. "Ah, this is what I mean. Most delicate. You know that Jean Beaulieu is a Communist *député* and Mayor of Chateau-Grignac?"

"Yes."

"The wrong word from you, the slightest insinuation, and the Minister would read about it on the front page of *L'Humanité.*"

"I know."

"I hope you do."

"We also plan to talk with Colonel Lebrun."

Aynard drew in his breath sharply. "A powder keg waiting to be detonated! Even the young Gaullists are afraid of the old man."

"I only intend to question him on what happened to the Réseau Renard. I'll keep away from politics."

"How can you? He thinks the Socialists are Communists and sees the Communists as agents of the devil. He wrote an open letter to Jacques Chirac not long ago accusing him of leftist tendencies."

"I'll be careful."

"See that you do. Now, what else?"

"We're running a national check on known hit men with the help of the Ministry. We've asked for some help from Interpol. London has offered their assistance. My people are out combing the underworld and we've alerted our informers."

"How about the members of McCallister's *réseau?*"

"They've all been questioned. Now we're investigating the background of each one of them personally. I'll be seeing them all again."

"Any suspicions?"

"No, but McCallister was not a hero to them."

The Commissaire pinched his nose and glanced at the wall clock. It was time for his meeting with the Préfet of Police.

"Well, now that I have explained everything carefully there should be no misunderstanding between us. Is that correct?"

"It is."

"Good," Aynard said, busying himself with the papers on his desk. "That will be all, Inspector."

Bastide was opening the door when Aynard called to him. "One thing, Inspector," he said, removing his glasses, "your personal life is—up to a point—your own. I am required to tell you, however, that your liaison with a certain woman could be professionally embarrassing. I think you know what I mean."

Bastide responded to Aynard, his chin raised. *"Monsieur le commissaire,* you are right. My personal life is my own. *Au revoir."* He shut the door firmly behind him.

Aynard scowled at the closed door. "Stubborn bull!" he murmured.

Inspector Bastide arrived in Toulon at noon and drove directly to Colonel Lebrun's villa. He was wearing his best suit and a knit tie. He had left his revolver at the office. The villa was perched high above the city on the Boulevard du Faron overlooking the harbor and the naval base. The colonel had insisted he come for lunch when Bastide had told him he would like to discuss the war and the Resistance. Bastide parked the Citroën, locked it and walked through a palm-shaded garden to the rounded door of the white stucco house. An elderly female housekeeper wearing scuffed slippers let him in. The hallway was dark after the bright sunlight outside. It took a moment for his eyes to adjust.

"The colonel is waiting for you," the old woman said. "Come." She led the way down the hall to a room at the back of the house and knocked softly.

"Entrez!" a parade-ground voice bellowed. The woman opened the door and gestured for Bastide to enter.

The colonel sat behind a Louis XV desk like a large-beaked bird ready to fly off at the slightest provocation. The dim light of the desk lamp accentuated his pallor and the sharp planes of his face. "Come in, come in, *monsieur l'inspecteur,"* the deep voice boomed. Bastide had the impression he was hearing a recording and not words from such a frail source.

"Bonjour, mon colonel, I . . ."

"Marie! A whiskey for the inspector," the colonel commanded.

Bastide sat down and looked around the room. It was a deeply shadowed museum of military memorablia. A stand of regimental flags spread behind the colonel giving the frail old bird a peacock's tail. The walls were hung with embossed Arab rifles, a buckler and crossed spears from Djibouti, a Tonkinese execution sword. The dun-colored tunic of an Afrika Korps captain was preserved in a glass case. It bore the Knight's Order of the Iron Cross. Bastide could see two bullet holes in the cloth surrounded by rusty blood stains.

The colonel tilted his head like a magpie. "Ah, you appreciate my souvenirs? A lifetime of service. That man," he said, jerking his nose toward the case, "was a good soldier. I put those bullets into him at Bir Hakim. An educated Prussian professional. I filled him with cognac and held his hand when he died, easing the painful process."

"That," the colonel said, pointing to the wall behind Bastide, "is where you'll find the material from the Resistance."

Bastide looked over his shoulder at a series of photos surrounding an old Sten gun.

"Didn't have much time to gather souvenirs then," the colonel commented. "The Boche kept us on the run."

Marie returned with a tray. She served Bastide a very dark whiskey without ice and put an open bottle of Perrier and an empty glass before the colonel. She slapped out the door in her loose slippers.

The colonel poured his Perrier with a trembling hand. "In my time I could have drunk you under the table, young man. Not now, not now." He sipped the sparkling water and looked at Bastide.

"Well, what can I tell you?"

"Have you heard of the death of the Englishman Mc-Callister?"

"I have," the colonel said shortly.

"I am working on the case. It is not easy. We need all the help we can get. I understand that your Resistance group was often in touch with the Réseau Renard?"

"Often? No, not often. As little as possible in fact. I do not know your politics, Inspector, nor will I ask you what they are. I will only say that the Réseau Renard was a disgrace to France. As, I might add, is our present government!"

At least the old bastard speaks his mind, Bastide thought, taking the first gulp of his drink and trying not to gasp. The whiskey was uncut by water.

"I can tell you that SOE, the British, were supporting that Socialist group as part of a plot." The colonel coughed. It brought a slight tinge of color to his cheeks but the color soon faded. "They wanted the Socialists in after the war, you see. They knew it would mean a weak, vacillating government in France. Then, they could get on with their plan to take over our colonies without trouble." The old man nodded, agreeing with himself. "You know," he continued, "I never did like De Gaulle, that pompous tyrant, but he did block the British after the war. That is the only good thing I can say for him."

"*Mon colonel*, did you meet McCallister during the war?"

"Once or twice. We had a dispute over some supplies.

Automatic rifles. Brens. They were dropped on our territory and I claimed them. He came over with that Campi clown and asked us to give them up to the Réseau Renard." The colonel chuckled. "I gave them five minutes to leave my headquarters area. They moved very fast."

"And another time?"

"It's hard to remember. Oh yes, it was a medical problem. One of my men had a bad belly wound. I'd heard that McCallister had studied pharmacy and asked him to come over and have a look before I risked contacting a doctor in Toulon. He did come. Told me the wounded man wouldn't live another twenty-four hours. He was right. McCallister had the real rank of captain, you know. Held a major's rank only for the duration of his time in France. I outranked him easily."

"The colonel is served," Marie announced from the hall.

"Ah, we shall eat now." The colonel had some trouble getting up from behind his desk, but he managed it with the help of a bamboo cane. Standing, he was even smaller than Bastide had imagined. "Come along, Inspector," he said, leading the way to the dining room.

They sat at a table of African ebony set with fine silver and crystal. Marie poured rosé from a cut-glass carafe before she served the first course of *artichaut vinaigrette.* She offered Bastide a piece of baguette from a silver *panier.* He could tell by the feel of the bread that it was at least a day old.

The colonel seemed to have sunk from sight at the other end of the table. Bastide could only see a few whisps of white hair protruding above the floral piece of red dahlias. A series of sucking and smacking sounds indicated the colonel was eating. Bastide took a mouthful. The artichoke had the consistency of overcooked mush. He decided his best tactic was to fill the air with questions.

"Who," he asked, "do you think might have killed McCallister?"

The colonel's sallow nose appeared above the dahlias. His eyes flashed. "The British!" the colonel bellowed as if Bastide had been a fool to pose the question.

"Why?" Bastide asked, slightly shaken. "Why would you say that?"

"It's simple. British Intelligence is everywhere. They have a long memory. They can't abide cowards. Now that the Conservatives are in power, they are cleaning out their kennels. They waited till McCallister left the country and *paf!* No McCallister."

Bastide sat back and sipped his rosé. His palate detected an acid blending of cheap Provençal and Spanish wines. He would have liked to put the colonel on a more reasonable road but he decided to hear him out.

"You think McCallister was a coward?"

"Of course. He ran from the fight. Left his Socialist comrades behind. Oh, it didn't last long. One look at those German parachutists and they soiled their pants and asked for mercy. The Germans were lucky. My group would have been an entirely different story. The fact remains, McCallister bolted. He was lucky his own people didn't shoot him."

"He was wounded though. The testimony says the FTP, the Communists found him the night after the attack."

"Those scum," the colonel growled, his mouth full of stale bread. "Beaulieu and his carrion. They were only there to gather up what arms or supplies might be lying around. You notice they didn't come running to help their Socialist 'comrades' when the fight was going on. They waited in safety till the firing died down and until they saw the *camions* come for the Germans. Then they appeared on the field like scavengers."

"But they did save McCallister's life."

The colonel snorted and rang a small glass bell to summon Marie.

She changed their plates and held a serving platter for Bastide. There was one piece of cold ham and one small boiled potato for each of them. Bastide took his share and Marie served the colonel.

"You won't overeat at my table, young man," the colonel commented. "I believe in lean stomachs and clear minds. No two-hour lunches in my mess."

Bastide chewed the salty ham, reflecting that it was fortunate he'd left Mattei in Marseille. When they had finished their lunch and Bastide had downed a ritual thimbleful of raw cognac he took his leave of the colonel. He was getting nowhere and the colonel had begun to doze off in his chair.

Marie saw him to the door. As the sound of Bastide's departing car reached the old man's study the colonel opened his rheumy eyes and pushed himself forward to lift the antique telephone off its brass receiver. He dialed a number and waited.

"Allo," he finally roared as if he were on a field telephone during a campaign, *"c'est moi, le colonel!* I have had my visitor. Yes, a mediocre fellow. This is what I require. I must know the politics of Inspector Roger Bastide. Yes, Police Judiciare of Marseille. As soon as possible."

Bastide drove down the winding street into Toulon

and thought of Mireille Perraud. She was only a short mile or two away. All he had to do was turn left on the Chemin de Forgentier. But he didn't. He passed it and headed for the autoroute to Marseille.

CHAPTER III

Mattei knew where to find JoJo le Lièvre. The Café des Colonies was off the Rue Roi René in the Lambert *quartier* of Marseille, squeezed between an old soap factory and a patisserie. The two metal tables on the sidewalk in front of the café were shaded by dirty blue-and-white umbrellas advertising a local vermouth and covered with dust and grime from the passing traffic. The bar itself was small, the walls decorated with amateurish murals depicting exotic scenes of South Sea islands, palms, banana trees and erupting volcanoes. The patron was a former inmate of Les Baumettes prison and most of his clients had either been there at one time or would find themselves within its walls in the future. To a stranger in search of a cool beer or an iced pastis, the Café des Colonies might have appeared an innocent watering hole oozing with local color. To the Marseille police it was bandit territory.

The long list of "events" that had occurred at the Café des Colonies provided a barometer for the violent storms and sudden calms of the Marseille underworld. The bar had been shut down on several occasions but the *patron* had paid his fines, proved his relative innocence and reopened the sun-bleached doors to his faithful customers. The last incident, in the spring of 1981, had seen the café closed for two weeks. Ange Sebastiani, one of the muscles in the Corso organization, and three of his "soldiers" had been playing an after-dinner game of belote at a table to the rear of the bar. Two young men had parked their motorbikes outside, walked into the café still wearing their cycling helmets and emptied the four barrels of their shotguns into Ange Sebastiani and his companions. They'd used heavy-bore shot and the sawed-off barrels had insured a wide spread. There had been no need for accuracy. It had taken the *patron* two days to clean and repaint the wall behind the table.

Inspector Babar Mattei parked his Mercedes a half block away and walked slowly toward the Café des Colonies. He unbuttoned his blazer and touched the reassuring solidity of the .38 on his right hip. As he approached the door he could hear a Tino Rossi record playing on the jukebox. Mattei was one of the few policemen who would think of entering the Café des Colonies without a backup. He had grown up in the *quartier*. His presence was tolerated but no more than that. Mattei walked in out of the sun like a heavyweight stepping into the ring. A mechanical smile creased his face and his eyes flicked from customer to customer.

"Tiens, tiens!" the *patron* commented without looking up, his hairy arms sunk in a basin full of dirty glasses, "Mattei *le magnifique.* What'll you have?"

Mattei's quick inventory was complete. Ramon Souche, a racetrack tout, at the far end of the bar; Bouche d'Or, an aging pimp, standing next to Souche; Georges Astier, a con man who preyed on tourists, suddenly fascinated with the juke box; and Mattei's target, JoJo le Lièvre, sitting alone at a table reading *Le Méridional* with a glass of beer in front of him. JoJo was ignoring Mattei's entrance.

"A Ricard," Mattei ordered, sighing and putting his two elbows on the bar. The *patron* poured the pastis and pushed a jug of water toward Mattei. He filled his glass and nodded toward Bouche d'Or.

"How's business?" he asked quietly.

Bouche d'Or shrugged. "Bad," he murmured, hoping that would end the conversation. He didn't like talking with cops.

"The Africans crowding you?"

Mattei knew the Senegalese were strengthening their hold on the edges of Bouche d'Or's territory, taking over lucrative strips of sidewalk for their own girls.

"There's room for everybody," Bouche d'Or replied unconvincingly.

"You be careful, *vieux,*" Mattei told him. "Those cannibals are not nice. They'll slice off your withered tool one of these nights and stuff it with rice. I wouldn't want to work on your case."

Bouche d'Or gulped his drink. He didn't laugh.

Mattei chuckled, picked up his glass and walked to JoJo le Lièvre's table. "*Bonjour,* Jo. Checking your stock market holdings?"

JoJo le Lièvre had a face the color of unbaked bread. His small eyes watched Mattei as he sat down facing the door. The Tino Rossi song ended. After a few clicks the Italian accent of Dalida began to thump through a Latin number. JoJo put his newspaper aside and lifted his beer, his eyes still on Mattei. JoJo was a middle-aged man with no apparent muscles. He seemed to be covered by an unexplicable coating of baby fat. His arms hung from his blue Lacoste sport shirt like two pink sausages and he wore an assortment of gold rings on the stubby fingers of his left hand.

Mattei sipped his pastis and leaned close to JoJo. "I've waited to hear from you for two days now," he said. "You were out of town. Or your maiden auntie was sick. Or didn't you get my message?"

"I planned to call you today. I . . ."

Mattei, still smiling, brought his shoe down hard on JoJo's instep. JoJo winced with pain. "Listen to me, you liar, when I want to talk to you, you jump! Understand?"

JoJo nodded his head and peered under the table at his injured foot.

Mattei leaned back in his chair and took a more moderate tone. "*Mon cher* Jo, you know you're indispensable. You have the biggest ears in Marseille. You hear everything, even the fart of a seagull passing the Château d'If. So, you see, we depend on you."

JoJo glanced around them uneasily. It was not good to be seen with Mattei in the Café des Colonies. Mattei diagnosed his problem.

"Oh, don't worry about your friends. Surely they wouldn't accuse you of talking business with me. They know I'm strictly homicide. Their small rackets don't interest us. But listen carefully with you ears fully opened. You've read of the Englishman who was murdered at Roucas?"

"Yes," JoJo replied.

"Good. I am working on the case. I must know if any of the 'families' were involved. He was killed by a professional. I don't know if he was a local or brought in from the outside. It may have nothing to do with your Marseille friends. If so, all the better." Mattei stopped talking. The Dalida record had ended. "You better play more music, Jo," Mattei suggested, "unless you want everyone to listen to us."

JoJo limped across the floor to the multicolored juke-box, poked a selection panel and came back to the table. A recording of "Ajaccio" filled the bar with brass.

"So, I expect you to circulate. Pick up all that you can. Clean the wax out of your ears. Call me tomorrow."

Mattei drank the last of his pastis and stood up. He put his empty glass on the bar and dropped some francs beside it. "Give my friend JoJo a cold beer," he told the *patron*.

"*Au revoir, les gars!*" he called over his shoulder as he walked out.

"*Salaud!*" Bouche d'Or cursed as Mattei disappeared from sight.

"*Salle flic!*" Ramon Souche muttered.

"Do you want the beer?" the *patron* asked JoJo le Lièvre.

"Not from that pig," JoJo replied, rubbing the blue bruise on his puffy foot.

Joseph Campi and Raoul Senac sat under the grape arbor behind Campi's farmhouse. There was a carafe of cool rosé, two half-filled glasses and a dish of small green olives on the table between them. Senac had his muscular arms folded across his chest. Campi's nose was a purple-hued rainbow from the wine and the sun.

"So you don't think it was one of ours?" Campi asked.

"I don't. What was to be gained?" Senac asked. "Look at us, you and me, for example. We are not young. The war was finished long ago. I detested McCallister for what he did. I hated him as much as anyone. I could have killed him with my bare hands if I'd found him in the German prison. But today? No, I thought of him as an-other human being with a certain weakness. You know,

Joseph, when he appeared at the cemetery it was strange, but I was glad to see him." Senac paused and glanced out across Campi's fields to the looming mountain of the Sainte-Baume. "He should have stayed in England," Senac said.

"He was good at his job," Campi commented, pouring more wine.

Senac agreed, smiling. "Do you remember our first jumps? What a comedy. There was a wind and you landed in a tree. McCallister drove his jeep by you on his way back to camp while you called for help like a lost kitten. When I asked about you he said, 'Let him get down himself. He may have to help himself when he drops into France.'"

Campi grinned. "The bastard," he recalled. "I had to cut the parachute harness and walk six miles. When I arrived you'd all gone to bed. He was drinking in his quarters. I was soaked to the skin and he poured me a glass of port. 'You owe His Majesty's government the price of a damaged harness,' he told me."

Campi shook his head. "I don't know," he went on. "I do not have your confidence in our comrades. You are much too reasonable. I recall Paradisi crying as the Boche trucked us into Toulon. I thought he was frightened and tried to comfort him. He wasn't afraid. He was angry with frustration. He told me he should have shot McCallister when he saw him leave the rocks. Did you see Paradisi at the cemetery? He had murder in his eyes."

"I cannot imagine anyone hiring a killer," Senac commented.

"It is an easy thing, you know," Campi suggested. "There are the others too."

"The others?"

"The colonel's people," Campi explained, "and Beaulieu and the Communists. You know how the colonel felt about McCallister. If he'd given the word in 1944, any number of his toy soldiers would have volunteered. McCallister, to them, was the living symbol of perfidious Albion. As to Beaulieu and his cocos, they were convinced that part of McCallister's job was to spy on them. I think they saw him as part of a capitalist plot to frustrate their plans and keep the Communists out of any postwar government."

Senac sighed. "It is all so complicated."

"Perhaps we will never know," Campi said.

"But surely, the police have their methods."

Campi snorted. "Oh, don't count on them. They will scratch and fuss till things have quieted down. Then some one at the top will tell them it's enough. I don't think they want to dig too deeply. Too much risk of unpleasant memories. Just imagine. If it was one of us. What would the Socialist Party have to say? And for the others the same." Campi laughed. "Can you imagine Député-Maire Beaulieu, the symbol of respectable, legal Communism in France, having to explain how a member of his Resistance group came to murder a former British officer in 1982? Or that old fool, the colonel, who has never forgiven the British for firing first at Fontenoy? He would probably become the hero of the extreme right!"

"Well," Senac said, looking up at the sun-dappled arbor, "McCallister's dead."

"Thirty-eight years," Campi mused, "and we're still killing each other."

A brown hunting dog made his way across the clods of the plowed field and flopped down at Campi's feet, panting. The cicadas buzzed around them and they could hear Campi's wife humming in the kitchen as she prepared the evening meal. Senac took an olive, chewed it and flicked the pit onto the ground.

Jean Beaulieu had been a member of the Assemblée Nationale and mayor of Château-Grignac for years. He was a gregarious, open-faced man. He owed his repeated reelection to office more to what he had done for the local farmers and farm workers than to any political attraction offered by the Communist Party. His wartime record as the efficient leader of the local Francs-Tireurs Partisans group had consolidated his popularity among his older constituents and his ability to squeeze funds from the government for municipal swimming pools and youth centers had endeared him to the younger generation. He knew his people well and took pains to distance himself from the more doctrinaire Communist officials of the region.

His May Day speeches concentrated on local problems and steered clear of polemics, national politics and international events. When he attended Party meetings in Paris he avoided being photographed with Georges Marchais, considering the bushy-browed leader of the French Communist Party too bellicose to be understood by the electors of Château-Grignac. Beaulieu dressed conservatively, covering his small frame with three-piece suits. He often ate lunch at his desk in the Mairie, a napkin tucked into his shirt collar, peering at his working files through thick, horn-rimmed spectacles and occasionally dripping salad dressing or red wine on his official papers.

The phone buzzed and the mayor picked it up. It was the owner of the Café de la Poste calling to tell him that the policeman had arrived and was eating lunch in the café. Beaulieu pulled his gold watch out of his vest pocket and snapped it open. "Very good, Martin," he said, "see that he eats well. He is due in my office after lunch. I think it would be wise to observe if he speaks with any one. If he asks any questions." Martin agreed and rang off.

Roger Bastide tasted his *blanquette de veau.* It was perfect. It never failed. Once you got out of the cities and into the small towns you could eat well for very little. He poured himself some wine from the carafe and it was surprisingly good too. His appointment with the mayor was for two-thirty. He had plenty of time. He had never met Député-Maire Beaulieu but he'd read a lot about him that morning. His war record was good. He'd obviously run his *maquis* with an iron hand and it had been an effective organization. They'd taken a lot of risks and killed a lot of Germans but, according to Beaulieu's dossier, it hadn't been without a heavy cost. One of their attacks on a German dispatch rider had brought swift reprisal in a small town north of Château Grignac. Six men, dragged out of the cafés and off the streets at random, had been shot by the Germans and dumped into the town's fountain. That community had never voted Communist after that.

Bastide helped himself to more *blanquette* from the covered casserole the young waitress had left on his table and thought about politics. He considered himself a good Republican in the French term of the word. Extremes of the Right or the Left made him angry and, although he had never been directly involved in politics, he had taken an active part in trying to keep political agitation out of the police force. He had seen the end result of political bankruptcy in Algeria and it had repelled him. He tended to lump all politicians together as bad fruit from the same tree. He knew it was a simplistic approach, but in his work he didn't have time for subtleties.

Bastide looked out of the café past the plane trees to the Mairie. The old sandstone building with a limp tricolor hanging from the balcony hardly looked like a Communist stronghold, but it was. He wondered where Beaulieu was lunching. Probably at some expensive nearby restaurant listed in the *Guide Michelin*. Well, he thought, his meal is certainly no better than mine.

As always, the Communists were well organized. When Jean Beaulieu finished his lunch and pushed the tray aside he reviewed the information on Inspector Roger Bastide provided by the Party cell in the Marseille police. Beaulieu was a methodical reader. Each fact registered in his mind with computerlike clarity. Antoine, Bastide's father, a fisherman at the Vallon des Auffes, had died in 1964. His mother, Marie, approaching eighty, now lives near Arles. Bastide visits her once a month. His brother, Eugène, works for a shipping company in Brest. His sister, Yvonne, is teaching at a *lycée* in Senegal. Beaulieu noted Bastide's one year at the University of Aix. He paid particular attention to the paragraph on military service.

Volunteering as a parachutist, Bastide had earned the Medaille Militaire in Algeria. But he had also been demoted from his rank of sergeant after protesting the methods used during a punitive expedition against a suspected fellagha village in the Aurès Mountains. That notation was interesting to Beaulieu. He read on, absorbing the salient details of Bastide's police career; his lack of political motivation and some brief comments on his relationship with Janine Bourdet. The report closed with the dry assessment that Bastide was an honest, professional policeman and, although he had shown signs of individualism during his Army service, it was doubtful if an effort to recruit him into the Party would be either successful or worthwhile.

"Violà," Beaulieu said to himself, slipping the report into a drawer of his desk as his intercom buzzed. His male secretary told him Bastide had arrived. He asked him to show Bastide in, brushed some crumbs off his vest and composed his face into a smile of greeting.

Bastide had done his homework too. The man who rose to shake his hand looked surprisingly like the photo stapled to the file Bastide had reviewed at the Hôtel de Police. Usually the portraits lacked a dimension that actually appeared when you met the subjects in the flesh. But Beaulieu matched his photo perfectly. This was the man who had personally tracked and shot the German Abwehr officer who had ordered the reprisal killings near Château-Grignac, the FTP leader who had ordered the hanging of two of his own men for the rape of a young farm girl during the Liberation, the Communist politician who had successfully defied every local and national political maneuver to remove him from office since his first election. He was also, Bastide thought, the man who might hold the secret to McCallister's death. The bland smiling face, the dark suit, the small belly, the gold watch chain, the horn-rimmed glasses all came together to form a perfect portrait of a bourgeois politician. Once the formalities were over and Bastide had begun to pose his questions he soon discovered why

Beaulieu had been so successful in politics. Time slipped by, the room was full of words and Bastide was learning nothing.

". . . those were exciting days," Beaulieu was reminiscing while he twirled his glasses in one hand. "The comradeship was something you don't forget. Have you ever served in the military, Inspector?"

"Yes. In Algeria," Bastide replied.

"Oh, that was different of course. A colonial war. But I do suppose you also had this feeling of closeness, of dependence on your friends."

"We did," Bastide agreed, glancing at the mantel clock behind the *député-maire*. Beaulieu seemed determined to stifle him in a web of pleasant chatter. The web had to be broken.

"Monsieur le député-maire," Bastide cut in, "is it possible that an ex-member of your organization could have killed McCallister?" The minute he'd spoken he remembered Aynard's warning: "The wrong word . . . the slightest insinuation . . . the front page of *L'Humanité* . . ."

The glasses stopped twirling. The pleasant smile lost much of its warmth. Beaulieu turned to Bastide, one eyebrow raised. "What a curious question!" he said. "Are you serious?"

"I am. You must understand; we have to explore every possibility. You know better than I that much happened during the summer of 1944. There was sacrifice and bravery but there was also hate and betrayal."

The smile was gone. The affable politician's portrait was being altered. The tough, wartime Resistance leader was slowly coming through the smooth veneer of sociability.

"You are asking me to accuse my comrades of murder? This is unthinkable! You are sitting here in the office of a member of the National Assembly and the mayor of the community of Château-Grignac and insinuating that a hero of the FTP might be an accomplice to a murder? *Monsieur l'inspecteur,* I must ask you to apologize."

Bastide felt a cool sweat on his forehead. He tried to explain.

"You have misunderstood," he said. "Our investigation must cover all involved. Joseph Campi and members of the Réseau Renard, Colonel Lebrun and his group and your FTP. Surely you can understand this necessity?"

"I only know that you are careless with your words," Beaulieu snapped.

"I do apologize if I have offended you," Bastide replied evenly, fighting a rising surge of anger. He knew Beaulieu was playing a role. He also knew he had to be careful or the veteran politician would lead him into a trap with no exit.

"Very well," Beaulieu said, "I accept your apology but I warn you, Inspector, no one, not even the President of the Republic, can come into my office and insult the memory of my comrades."

Bastide cleared his throat and tried a more indirect approach.

"Allow me to ask a question to which I do not think you can object."

Beaulieu nodded. "Please do."

"Do you, on the basis of your wartime experience, think that the McCallister murder was linked with his role in the Resistance?"

Beaulieu was silent for some time. He replaced his

glasses slowly, settling them on the bridge of his nose.
"Yes," he said, "it is very possible. But that is only my
personal opinion, an unofficial estimate."

"You understand, *Monsieur le député-maire*, that I will be
speaking with members of your wartime organization as
part of the routine investigation."

"Oh yes, Inspector, I do," Beaulieu replied, a faint
smile making its reappearance. "But allow me to make a
suggestion. I would be very careful of my choice of
words. We Communists are not all thick-skinned mili-
tants, you know. Some of us can be very sensitive."

Inspector Mattei shook hands with the Englishman
and they all sat down.

"It is too bad Inspector Bastide is not available," Commissaire Aynard said. "Inspector Mattei will be able to
help you get settled."

Mattei had been caught off balance by the *commissaire's*
summons, but he smiled at the Englishman reassuringly.

"Monsieur Napier has come to solve some of the insurance problems involving the McCallister murder for
the British Consulate General," he told Mattei. "I have
told the consul general he can expect full cooperation
from us."

Mattei watched the Englishman as he spoke, explain-
ing his plans and thanking the *commissaire* for his consid-
eration. There was something about him that put a doubt
in Mattei's mind. He didn't look like an insurance expert
or a lawyer. More like a fellow cop. He had a florid
complexion and a bristling white mustache. His blue
eyes were alert and bright peering through the clouds of
smoke erupting from his pipe. There seemed to be a
smile lurking just beyond his thin lips. Mattei sensed the

Englishman had already classed Commissaire Aynard as a pompous sham.

Mattei was right on both counts. Mr. Colin Napier was not a lawyer or a legal expert. He was a professional intelligence officer who had left MI6 headquarters in London that morning after a thorough briefing on the McCallister case and "Operation Red Gold." Napier had also made an instantaneous decision that the less he saw of Commissaire Aynard while in Marseille the better. He liked neither Aynard's unctuous manner in addressing him nor the obvious off-handedness with which he addressed the stocky Mattei.

"So, gentlemen," the *commissaire* told them, "I shall let you both go. Mattei can bring you up to date in his office. Bastide should be back soon."

Once the two men had left him alone, Aynard opened his drawer, fumbled with a tube of medicine and popped a tablet into his mouth. His wife had invited an official from the Préfecture and his wife to dinner. The *commissaire* groaned audibly thinking of the thick, rich sauces their Spanish cook had undoubtedly prepared.

Mattei led the visitor to Bastide's office.

"Take a chair," Mattei said.

The Englishman smiled. "I would rather stand," he replied in fluent French. "I have been sitting on the plane all morning."

"Oh, yes. As you please." Mattei saw some telephone messages on Bastide's desk. "Excuse me," he said, reading through them hurriedly. Routine calls on the whole. The last message came from the Police Maritime and was marked URGENT. The Englishman walked to the window, shaded his eyes from the sun and looked at the Cathedral. Mattei dialed the number of his friend Fabré at the headquarters of the Police Maritime.

"*Allo*, Jacques Fabré, if you please."

The Englishman turned from the window and gestured toward the Cathedral. "Most impressive," he said.

Mattei nodded. The Englishman was obviously without any taste in architecture.

"Fabré here!"

"It's Mattei. What is so urgent, Jacques? Did your *lascars* find a Roman galley full of amphora?"

"Very amusing, Babar. No, it's a *machabée*. Watersoaked and coated with crabs. We fished him out near the Pointe Rouge. He's one of yours I'm afraid."

"One of ours?"

"Yes, imbecile. A murder. Neck almost severed by a piano wire garrote. Only the vertebrae holding him together."

"*Ah, merde!*"

"Exactly. Now you'll have to put down your girlie magazine and go to work."

"Any identification?"

"Bare as a cleaned sardine. But he does have a tatoo. The word COMMANDO under an anchor of *la coloniale*. Can you people pick him up? He's stinking up our dock."

"Look, I have a visitor and Bastide is not here. Can't you call the morgue?"

"Done, *mon vieux*. Always ready to help my landbound colleagues."

"Thanks. I'll buy you a drink . . . soon."

"Miracle of miracles, that's worth a phone call."

Mattei made a quick call to put someone on the case of the garroted commando. Then he turned his attention to the Englishman, apologizing for keeping him waiting.

Napier, still puffing smoke like an ancient locomotive, put his hand on Mattei's broad shoulder. "I suggest we seek the cool air of a café terrace," he said. "I would like you to be my guest."

Mattei needed no urging to leave the hot office. He led Napier out of the Hôtel de Police and drove him to the Vieux Port. They settled on the crowded terrace of La Samaritaine.

An African vendor, spotting Napier as a foreigner, homed in on their table. He was laden with badly carved ebony and ivory artifacts. He pushed a walking stick toward Napier. "Very cheap," he pleaded, "only two hundred francs."

"Walk, little father!" Mattei snapped, "or you'll never see Abidjan again." There was enough authority in Mattei's tone to ring an alarm bell. The vendor moved on.

The Englishman ordered a double gin and asked for a bottle of Angostura bitters. Mattei settled for a draft beer. When their drinks came the Englishman let a few drops of bitters slide down the inside of his glass and whirled the gin around till the bitters had been absorbed.

"You don't want any ice?" Mattei asked.

"No, no, this is just fine. To your health."

They drank, toasting each other. Mattei asked how he could be of help. Napier wanted to know about the actual death of McCallister. Mattei began a long monologue broken only by understanding mumbles and an occasional question from the Englishman. He seemed interested in the members of the Réseau Renard, particularly in the life style of each veteran. Mattei found he couldn't answer many of the questions. The investigation hadn't dug that far yet. He looked at Napier out of the corner of his eye. The pipe was still emitting wisps of smoke, the blue eyes were taking in everything on the terrace and he was on his third double.

"*Drôle de type!*" Mattei thought. "He'll be rubber-legged by the time we leave the café." He swallowed the last of his beer. "Can I drop you at your hotel?" Mattei asked.

"No, thank you. I think I'll just sit here and enjoy the sunset."

Before he left, Mattei gave Napier both his office and home telephone number. Much later, on his way home to dinner, Mattei drove past La Samaritaine and glanced at the terrace. The Englishman was still there. In fact, as Mattei waited for the traffic light to change he could see he was ordering another drink.

JoJo le Lièvre heard about the body brought in by the Police Maritime while he was eating a pizza at a cheap restaurant on the Quai du Port. He wiped some grease from his chin and listened more carefully. The fisherman who'd reported the floating corpse to the police was embellishing his tale with gestures, telling the barman how the police launch had to make two passes before they secured the body.

"I could have reached out and grabbed it," the fisherman said, "but the cops told me to stand off. They floundered past and left such a wake they almost sent the corpse to the bottom."

Two other customers chuckled and nodded in agreement. Any discomfiture suffered by the police was amusing to them. "How do you know it was a murder?" one of them asked.

The fisherman put down his glass of white wine and made a quick strangling gesture. "Wire . . . around the neck. Disgusting. A few more hours in the water and there wouldn't have been a head."

"Can they identify the poor bastard?" the barman asked.

"I had to pull up over at the police landing to give a statement. They'd laid the corpse out on the dock. Naked as a newly born. There was a tattoo on one arm. COMMANDO . . . that's all it said, you know, with a kind of anchor. The crabs had done such a job you could hardly see it. Don't serve me *crabe mayonnaise* for a year!"

JoJo le Lièvre chewed his pizza and frowned. He was thinking, reaching back into his memory for a fragment of information he knew was there. Somewhere, sometime, there had been a tattoo much the same as that described by the fisherman. He knew he should be concentrating on Mattei's needs but his experience had taught him that every overheard conversation, every minute bit of intelligence was worth storing for possible future use.

A hiccup shook his massive body. He took three gulps of beer. The harder he thought the more irritated he became with himself for not producing an answer. It was there somewhere, wreathed in a mental fog. He concentrated on the word "commando." A filmlike sequence of images passed through his mind, all linked to the word "commando." Commandos in World War II; parachute commandos in Indochina; commando veterans at a ceremony in Paris; a brutal policeman he remembered with loathing who had been a commando. He rejected them all.

Then he linked the anchor, the sea, with the word. Marine . . . marine commando. He was getting somewhere now. He could feel it. An image slowly came into focus. He was sitting with three other men in an old *mas* behind Bandol. One of them had handed him an envelope full of hundred-franc notes for information he had supplied on the corruptibility of a bank guard. His information had proved correct. Their operation had been a success. Two of the men he'd known for years. The third was a newcomer and he'd asked about him. "That is Lucien Brannec," one of the others had whispered. "A tough little Breton, just out of the Navy with a dishonorable discharge. He comes highly recommended. He could shoot the nipples off a flat-chested whore at two hundred meters." How long ago had it been. JoJo le Lièvre popped the last hunk of pizza into his mouth. Almost five years. He got up slowly and moved to the bar next to the fisherman.

"Another beer," he told the barman, "and another drink for my friend here. He must have a dry throat from talking."

The fisherman grinned and pushed his empty glass across the bar for a refill. "I hope I didn't spoil your dinner," he said.

"No, I've heard worse," JoJo replied. *"Santé,"* he said, raising his glass of beer.

"À la votre," the fisherman reciprocated.

"Tell me," JoJo asked, "the dead one . . . was he small?"

"Ah, yes, very small. Not much of a commando."

JoJo smiled. Now his mind was racing. He carried on a desultory conversation at the bar but all his mental effort was shifting facts and weighing alternatives. An Englishman with his head blown off. A murdered sharpshooter pulled out of the water days later. The police would be very interested. They could wait. Someone else might be even more interested in his deduction.

CHAPTER IV

Hugo Paradisi agreed to drop by Inspector Bastide's office on his way home from the docks. It meant Bastide would have to wait till 7 P.M. but he wanted to finish his questioning of the Réseau Renard. He'd already talked again to the others. They seemed clean, but each had been surprisingly reticent or forgetful about what had happened in 1944 on the morning of the German attack. Bastide could understand that no one enjoyed talking about a defeat, but he knew something was being held back, something that could have a direct bearing on McCallister's murder. Not one of them had been able to explain how McCallister had avoided capture by the Germans when the position was overrun.

Senac had mumbled something about the Englishman being well hidden. Campi said he himself was stunned after a grenade exploded nearby and didn't see anything. Colbert thought McCallister had gone for a medical kit to treat the British sergeant. Duverger and Blanchard said they were too busy avoiding machine-gun fire to see anything. Bastide thought about each man. They were all solid types . . . at least on the surface. Family men with farms or businesses or good positions in established companies. Campi and Duverger were still active in the Socialist Party and friends of Marseille's long time Socialist mayor. Now that France had a Socialist President there was talk that Duverger might be called to Paris to fill a minor post in the Ministry of Defense.

Bastide flicked through his notebook. Nothing leapt out as extraordinary. A police wagon klaxoned its way along the Place de la Major and a coastal freighter blew a long, mournful farewell to the city as it passed the Digue Sainte-Marie. Bastide paused and backtracked a few pages in his notebook. He'd seen the name Paradisi buried in Blanchard's testimony. "A very successful man," Blanchard had commented at one point when asked about Paradisi's shipping company.

Bastide dropped the notebook on his desk and yawned. It was almost seven. He would have to get up to Arles to see his mother soon. He was sure she was doing too much in the garden and he wanted to hire a young boy to help her with the fruit trees and the vegetables. He also knew he would hear another lecture on the spiritual benefits of returning to the Church and the need for him to find a wife. As each year passed the lectures became more frequent and rambling but her genius in the kitchen hadn't changed. He remembered his last visit and the *grives aux olives*. The tender birds had been flavored with juniper berries and thyme, sautéed in light olive oil and served on fried toast surrounded by the tiny black olives from the grove behind the house. A pure symphony.

A uniformed policeman tapped on the open door. Hugo Paradisi stood beside him. Bastide welcomed him and pulled up a chair. Paradisi was smoking a dark cheroot and perspiring from his climb up the stairs. He wiped his face with a clean handkerchief and waited expectantly for Bastide to speak.

"Monsieur Paradisi," Bastide began, "I am pleased you could come today."

"It is nothing."

"I have spoken to your friends. Everyone has been most cooperative."

Paradisi acknowledged Bastide's comment with a nod and blew a smoke ring toward the ceiling.

"I am afraid no one," Bastide continued, "has an idea or even a slight suspicion as to who might have killed McCallister. Is there anything you've remembered, anything that happened in 1944 or later, that might have a bearing on the murder?"

Paradisi put his hands on his knees and looked Bastide in the eye. *"Monsieur l'inspecteur,"* he said quietly, "I have a confession to make."

Bastide's look of surprise brought a smile to Paradisi's swarthy face. "No, I am not going to confess to McCallister's murder. My confession is of a crime that might have been. That day on the ridge I would have killed him myself if I had been a bit more decisive. You see, I saw him leave our position. I couldn't understand it . . . thought I was mistaken. But there he was, slipping away and running down the slope, leaving us to face the Boche. I had a few precious seconds to drop him like a rabbit and . . . I didn't do it."

Bastide smoothed his mustache, thinking. "And the others. Did they have the same chance?"

"You've talked to them. It is for them to answer that question. But it is likely I was the only one to see him run. I was closer to him."

"What was your feeling when you heard he'd survived?"

"I was angry. But that was after V–E Day. Since then . . ." Paradisi shrugged.

"How did it feel to see him again the day of the ceremony?"

"It was a bad experience. All the old poisons coming to the surface. I hated him again."

"But not enough to . . ."

Paradisi shook his head. "No. I had almost forgotten him. Seeing him again just upset me. Seeing him dead a short time later brought me no joy. A body without life is sad."

"You know that McCallister was wounded when Beaulieu's people found him?"

"Yes, I do."

"Are you sure you did not make a decision that morning and pull the trigger?"

"I did not. If I had, I assure you he would not have lived."

"Why do you suppose the FTP didn't come to your assistance during the fight?"

Paradisi smiled and stubbed his cheroot out in the ashtray on Bastide's desk. "A difficult question. If you are expecting a political answer, you will be disappointed. I have never gotten along with the *cocos* but they did a good job during the war. I believe most of what Beaulieu said about the incident. You see, a partisan's job is to work quietly and secretly without drawing attention. The Germans would have liked nothing better than to draw both the FTP and the colonel's *maquis* into the fight. But Beaulieu and the colonel were not fools. They did not play the heroes or the German's game."

"The colonel says the Communists arrived after the fight to pick up what was left on the field."

Paradisi opened his hands wide. "Why not? We would have done the same. London was not overly generous with its supplies."

Bastide went back to his notebook and covered most of the ground he had been over with Paradisi's comrades. After twenty minutes he tossed the notebook aside. "One last question," he said. "Was there anything strange in McCallister's behavior just before the action? Anything unusual?"

Paradisi pursed his lips. "There was the drop that night . . ."

"Your friends mentioned it. Some arms parts?"

"Yes, that was it. McCallister and the British sergeant were the reception committee."

"None of you were there?"

"No, there was no need. A single canister. We had plenty to do installing ourselves on the ridge. They brought the canister back at dawn, just as I went off sentry duty."

"Nothing unusual?"

"No."

"Well," Bastide said, getting up and extending his hand. "Thank you. I may bother you again. You are not leaving on vacation?"

"No, my business won't allow it. I take my vacations in the spring."

"I envy you. Can you find your way out?"

"Yes, *au revoir.*"

It was eight-thirty by the time Bastide left the Hôtel de Police. He called the switchboard and said he planned to stop for an apéritif at Chez Caruso. It was a warm night and he decided to walk down the hill past the Fort Saint-Jean to the Vieux Port. There was no reason for him to take a police vehicle. One of these days he planned to buy a used car but he could borrow Janine's Peugeot when he needed it. He remembered Aynard's warning. The Breton had a long nose. He laid the blame for the *commissaire's* comments on Aynard's wife. She specialized in other people's lives. For her, his relationship with Janine was a juicy piece of scandal, a subject for continued gossip. It was lucky for him that Janine's milieu daunted the *commissaire's* wife and her doxies.

He passed the Fort Saint-Jean and turned left along the Quai du Port. Most of the café terraces were full. He could smell the odor of grilled fish and garlic.

Most of the terrace tables at Chez Caruso were occupied by diners but he found an empty spot and sat down. The illuminated spire of Notre-Dame de la Garde rose above the dancing lights of the harbor and some bright stars seemed to form a new halo over the statue of *"la bonne mère."* He ordered a pastis and was about to enjoy it when Mattei's dented green Mercedes swung into the curb beyond the terrace. Mattei climbed out, locked his door and waved. Bastide could see his assistant was both hot and thirsty.

"Bon sang!" Mattei said, falling into a seat. "What a day."

"It is not over, my friend," Bastide told him. "You've just parked in a no-parking zone."

Mattei ignored the comment. He signaled the waiter to bring him what Bastide was drinking. "I've been at the morgue trying to clear up that garrote murder. Still don't know who it was. No one's claimed the body. Looks like a gang hit to me."

"The dead commando?"

"Well, that's what the tattoo says. Who knows?"

"Sounds like it might have a link with the Foreign Legion. Did you try them?"

The waiter served Mattei's pastis. He sipped it before answering. "No, but it's an idea. I've put someone on the case. In any event, it's of little interest. Let me tell you about the Englishman."

"I saw your note."

"It only told half the story. He is a caricature; a true Major Thompson. Bushy mustache, white eyebrows bouncing around and drink . . . unbelievable! He must have gone through half a bottle of gin while we were at La Samaritaine."

"He is an insurance inspector?"

"I'm not sure. Something of that sort. He's come to assist the British Consulate so I presume he's traveling on an official passport. But something is not right. It's the way he asks questions."

"That's his business."

"No, there's something else. The moment I saw him I said to myself, 'Babar, this fellow isn't in insurance.' Later I was sure of it. I think he's a British *poulet*. One of us. Incidently, he speaks excellent French . . . almost too well."

Bastide thought for a minute. Mattei could be right. He was a street-wise cop with good, natural instincts. But why would the English be sending a policeman without consulting us or the Minister of the Interior? Bastide reflected on the McCallister case and its wartime associations. The words of a friend, an officer in the DST, came back to him: "Some of the consulates in Marseille have their quota of intelligence officers. They don't even know how to stamp a visa. Most of them are harmless, but we keep our eyes on them."

"We may have an aging James Bond on our hands," Bastide suggested.

Mattei shrugged. "If he enjoys women as much as he does gin, he'll be too exhausted to give us any trouble. By the way, how did it go with Paradisi?"

"I think he's an honest man."

"Oh?"

"Yes, he admitted having wanted to kill McCallister."

Mattei sat up in his seat. "That is interesting!"

"But it was during the war."

"Still interesting."

"Yes, I agree."

They enjoyed their drinks in silence for a moment, watching the steady passage of tourists, peanut vendors and families seeking a reasonable restaurant. Fathers and mothers stopped to read the sidewalk menus, commented on the dishes and hesitated at the prices while their children pulled impatiently to be off or stared at the plates of the nearby diners.

"Babar," Bastide said suddenly, "do you recall there was an airdrop on the night before the German attack?"

"Yes, most of them mentioned it in passing. A routine matter, according to them."

"Maybe, but it seems strange that only the two Englishmen went out to receive it."

"Oh, I asked one of them. I think it was Blanchard. He told me they all took turns when it wasn't a heavy delivery."

Bastide put his head back and looked up at the sky. "According to what I read in our interrogation notes the airdrop was due at two A.M."

"Correct."

"Paradisi says the two Englishmen didn't return with

the canister until dawn . . . when he was going off guard duty."

"Well, the drop was some distance from their position."

"Not that far."

Mattei ordered a refill and told the waiter to bring them a plate of shrimp grilled over fennel. The waiter was new. He told them he could serve them dinner but not an individual plate as an appetizer.

Mattei put his heavy hand on the waiter's forearm. "My dear friend," he said quietly, "you tell the boss that Inspector Mattei would like a plate of grilled shrimp. I am sure it will be no problem." The waiter freed himself and scuttled off to the interior of the restaurant.

"Babar," Bastide said reprovingly, "enough of that heavy business."

Mattei chuckled. "Politeness and charm gets one nowhere in today's world."

"I plan to eat at La Mère Pascal," Bastide said. "I don't want to ruin my appetite with grilled shrimp."

"*Tant pis.* I can eat them all."

Bastide reached across and readjusted the bottom of Mattei's sport coat. "Your cannon is showing," he told him.

"Oh, sorry. Maybe that's what moved the waiter."

"Do you sleep with it too?"

"Almost. I believe in protection."

Bastide shook his head. "The least you can do is carry something smaller."

"Now you're talking like a lot of dead cops I used to know," Mattei replied. "I've never understood your attitude, Roger. Here you sit as bare as a baby's ass. How do you know who you'll run into tonight? Or who might be waiting for you in the shadows near your apartment?"

"I carry one occasionally," Bastide replied.

"I'd feel better if you went around with your piece in a hand purse like those characters in narcotics. At least you could beat someone to death with it."

The waiter returned with the plate of shrimp, a panier of bread, two napkins and a fingerbowl. He put the plate down with a flourish and served it with their pastis.

"You see," Mattei chided him, "that was not difficult."

"No, *monsieur l'inspecteur.* I shall recognize you now. Would you like some mayonnaise?"

"Yes, that would be perfect."

Mattei reached for a large shrimp, cracked its shell and removed the tail meat intact. "Dig in," he told Bastide. "They are fresh, tender and perfectly grilled."

Bastide leaned over to tap him on the shoulder. "Before you start eating, *mon cher,* I suggest you do something about that." He pointed to Mattei's car. A traffic policeman with one foot on the Mercedes' rear bumper was writing out a ticket.

"Espèce de couillon!" Mattei exploded, vaulting out of his chair, leaving Bastide laughing on the terrace.

Bastide did help Mattei eat the shrimp. Then they said good-night and Bastide walked around the port to La Mère Pascal, picking up a copy of *Le Soir* on the way. He called the office and settled down to dinner. The last of Dominique's *plat de jour,* the breast of veal stuffed with artichokes and peas, had been served. Bastide settled for a tender slice of veal liver prepared with capers, parsley and garlic and a salad. He ordered a half bottle of red from Bandol, opened his paper and began to read the sports page.

The cats of Château-Grignac gathered after midnight in the Place de la Mairie after rummaging through the refuse bins of the town's shuttered restaurants and cafés. The few street lights winked through the foliage of the plane trees at the yellow-striped, black and gray felines as they cleaned their sticky paws or tangled in brief, noisy clashes. Their eyes momentarily reflected the head lights of cars speeding through the village on their way to the autoroute. The more seasoned toms stationed themselves near a smelly culvert waiting for a plump rat to emerge.

Député-Maire Jean Beaulieu was still in his office, finishing a speech he was to give in three days at a Communist rally to raise money for *L'Humanité,* the Party newspaper. He had received a polite but firm reminder from Party headquarters that this speech was to include references to national and international politics. Someone in Paris had tired of his constant concentration on events in his own backyard. He was finding it hard to complete a paragraph without wanting to sink his rhetorical teeth into the Socialists. He had known it would be difficult for his Party once a Socialist was in the Élysées Palace. He had not known how difficult. He put down his pen and tugged at his watch chain. He flipped open the lid of his gold watch and sucked in his breath. Almost two in the morning! He picked up his pen and made another effort but the words wouldn't come. He tried to pick up his previous rhythm, reading over the finished pages.

"We stand alone," he read, "deserted by those who once called us comrades. Alone against the forces of the right and the vacillations of a government that has neither the ability or the courage to govern France. We stand alone and threatened by the growing power of a reactionary America . . ." He paused to cross out "reactionary," replacing it with "dominant"; it still didn't sound right. ". . . a dominant America interested only in multinational profit and the rape of Third World resources."

Beaulieu put his pen down again, raised his spectacles to his forehead and rubbed his eyes. A cat howled out in the Place. He got up, walked to an antique cabinet inlaid with mother-of-pearl and opened the curved doors. He filled a small crystal glass with cognac from a bottle of Rémy Martin. The cognac burned his lips but it tasted good. There was no use going home tonight. He would sleep on the divan in his office. It wouldn't be the first time. His wife would understand. He could finish the speech in the morning when he was comparatively fresh.

He walked to the window and stood there thinking of Inspector Bastide's visit. The damn Englishman! Why did he have to come back to die in France after all those years? Normally Beaulieu could have finished the speech easily within an hour. Not now. He didn't want to admit it but he sensed a threat in the air. A feeling of impending disaster. He poured himself more cognac and began to pace back and forth over the shining parquet floor. Was it possible that all he had built since the war could now be threatened? He shook his head, trying to tell himself he was a nervous fool but the self-reassurance failed miserably. Surely every man was allowed one mistake in his life? Each of his questions hung there unanswered. He was enough of a realist to know people weren't allowed mistakes or chances according to some universal plan. They took or they gave; they lost or they won; and that was that. The cognac went down smoothly. Without really noticing it he had poured himself a third glass.

Suddenly tired, he walked behind his desk and sat down heavily. His eyes swept over his office. It was eighteenth-century, with a rose-marble fireplace and a crystal chandelier but it was sparsely furnished. Only the antique cabinet looked as if it belonged there. When he'd first been elected he'd moved out the old furniture and had it stored. Communist mayors had to set an example. His desk, his chair and the other furnishings were utilitarian, drab and out of place in the ornate setting but they suited his staff and the Party members. He didn't want his constituents to feel they were walking into the court of Louis XVI when they visited him. He looked at the photos placed along the mantelpiece. He was too far away to see them clearly but he knew each one by heart. An old photo showing him thin and young next to a grinning Thorez; crowded in among other Party leaders during an Algerian war protest march on the Champs-Élysées; standing under a Confédération Générale du Travail banner during an agricultural strike at Peyrolles and alone at the entrance to the National Assembly on the day he entered as a *député* for the first time. There were others too, most of them taken in Château-Grignac: speeches, bicycle races, outdoor lunches. The record of his career.

And now? Fate and a dead Englishman could ruin everything. He took a key ring from his pocket, selected a small key and opened the small right-hand drawer of his desk. It was stuffed with old letters, notes, loose paper clips, a book on the life of Fidel Castro signed and presented to him by its French author, an intellectual from Aix. He rummaged through the mess until he uncovered a small, red-leather jewel box. He put it on the desk, pushed the release and the top sprang open. The box contained souvenirs of the war: folded citations from the French government, a Croix de Guerre with two palms from his post-Resistance service with the French Army in Alsace and a murky photo of himself shaking hands with a tall American parachute captain after the action at Le Muy. He spilled it onto the desk and reached under the layer of cotton batting at the bottom of the box till his fingers found what he wanted. The gold napoleon caught the light as he lifted it to his eyes. The coin had become a very dangerous souvenir.

Colin Napier was up early and had his tea on the hotel terrace overlooking the narrow entrance to the Vieux Port. He could tell it was going to be a scorcher. The sun had already dissipated whatever coolness had been left from the early morning. It hung over the blue sea like a fiery orange and Napier could feel its sting on his cheeks. He finished the last of his croissant, flicked the crumbs off the lapels of his cotton suit, lit his pipe and left a tip for the waiter. It was still too early to appear at the Consulate so he walked down the hill slowly, enjoying the views of Marseille.

He stopped when he reached the high stone walls of the Fort Saint-Nicolas and peered at the entry gate of the Foreign Legion recruiting depot. A Legion sentry with Slavic cheekbones stood in the shade, his white kepi tilted over his eyes, his scarlet epaulets sagging on his shoulders. Napier wondered how many Englishmen had passed through those gates in the past year. Not many, he would guess. The days of Beau Geste were over . . . if they ever existed. A stocky adjutant in a sharply pressed uniform came out of the guardhouse, saw Napier and paused to stare back at him.

Napier nodded. "How goes the Legion, *mon adjutant?*" he asked, smiling.

The adjutant shrugged. "Slowly, monsieur," he replied, "very slowly."

Napier walked on, pausing to inspect the yachts berthed at the yacht club. A few large ketches and yawls with spotless decks and brightly polished brass were tied up close to the club house. An American ensign hung from one varnished stern. Two of the others were under Panamanian registry. By the time he reached an empty taxi stand he was perspiring. He crossed the street to a café, found a spot at the bar between two coffee drinkers and ordered a gin and orange. The barman almost made a joke about gin so early in the morning but saw his customer was a foreigner and decided to hold his tongue. Napier emptied his glass, paid, and hurried across the street to hail the cab that had just pulled into the stand.

Napier had to admit that his welcome by the British Consul General was something less than cordial. The CG was obviously a Foreign Office fuddy-duddy impressed by his title, a title that Napier happened to know had been very slow in coming and had only been bestowed as a sop to the CG's imminent retirement from the service. He was also a nonsmoker as Napier had surmised by his repeated, unsubtle attempts to wave away Napier's pipe smoke. He'd classed the CG along with Commissaire Aynard as types he would avoid while in Marseille.

Napier did succeed in having an empty office allotted to him and, after locking the door, he turned his attention to the special diplomatic bag that had been waiting unopened for his arrival. His white eyebrows rose and fell as he struggled with the seal, the lock and the leather fastenings. Bloody medieval methods he reflected, finally forcing the bag open and spilling its contents onto a desk. He put the empty bag aside, relit his pipe and began to sort things out. His own leather notebook was there, an important working tool. It contained a weird calligraphy of symbols, notes and squiggles, his own personal shorthand reminding him of important aspects of the McCallister case, Operation Red Gold and the prime objectives of his task in France—of making one more attempt to recover the gold and doing his best to keep the details of the operation from becoming known. There were no names, dates or places listed and a cipher expert could have spent the rest of his life trying to make sense out of Napier's mosaic with no hope of success.

He slipped the notebook into the inside pocket of his rust-colored jacket and picked up three thick files secured with buckled canvas straps. These were his "cover" files, the material he was supposed to be working with in regard to the legal aspects of McCallister's murder. They were labeled RESTRICTED but he piled them neatly at one corner of the desk. The last item was a long, rectangular box, tightly sealed with heavy tape. Napier sat down behind the desk and began to work on the tape with a letter opener, frowning with his effort. It finally popped open. Napier reached into the cotton batting and produced a bottle of Bombay gin. He dusted the bottle off, put it on the table and pulled a small package out of the open box. The package was stained with grease. He unfolded the paper carefully to reveal the dull sheen of a small .25-caliber Browning automatic with an extra clip taped to its grip. He pursed his lips and

glanced around the office. The safe was in one corner.
The CG had given him the combination but Napier
would have to change it. He expected someone would
snoop sooner or later and he didn't want the CG to die of
apoplexy on finding his insurance expert had come to
Marseille armed.

It was an old safe, one of the cheap Dartmoors produced after the war. A solid cough could open it. The
tumblers were so off kilter it took Napier an inordinate
amount of time to change the combination. When he'd
finished he wiped his face with a linen handkerchief and
looked around the office for a glass. No luck. He unscrewed the top of the gin, nodded his respects to the
grim faced Empress of India on the label and downed a
generous jolt. He put his dead pipe aside and drew a
clean one from his pocket. He sat down again, filled the
bowl with tobacco and made a slow ritual of lighting it.
When the white smoke curled toward the ceiling he
leaned back to do some thinking.

Operation Red Gold had been a balls-up. One of many
in the SOE's "war of the shadows." Most of them had
died the natural death reserved for official failures. Red
Gold would have remained forgotten in the graveyard of
dated dossiers if the McCallister case hadn't come up.
Napier narrowed his eyes, reviewing the facts carefully in
his mind. He tried to keep his thoughts factual, cold and
to the point but he found himself adding dashes of his
own editorial commentary.

Some SOE official with experience and contacts with
the Communist Francs-Tireurs Partisans had sold London on their discipline and effectiveness as Resistance
fighters. He had reasoned that London should drop their
misgivings about FTP politics and insure that FTP units

were given the proper support in arms, equipment and funds. After all, he had argued, thousands of tons of supplies were pouring into the Soviet Union and the Allied navies were taking heavy casualties delivering them on the Murmansk run. Why should there be any hesitation as far as the FTP's needs? Napier cocked his head to one side. Well, he had been right up to a point. But there was a big difference between helping the Soviets, who were tying down innumerable German divisions on the Eastern front, and assisting an armed Communist entity in France. Particularly since no one was sure of their postwar objectives.

The proposal was then taken up at a very high level. Enter an old intelligence professional in nasty doings, a latter-day Machiavelli. According to what Napier had read, this gentleman suggested headquarters go along with the plan. He also convinced them that it would be most interesting to attempt to "turn" a selected FTP Resistance leader in the process. His argument was well-prepared and convincing. He had sketched the profile of the man they were looking for. A Communist with ambition, one who knew that success and fame in the Resistance would provide a ticket to political prominence and personal stature.

If such a man could be found and if he could be "turned," SOE would have a model operation that could be used on others, thus providing a small but helpful *réseau* within the French Communist party. The thought of such an intelligence bonanza in an unstable postwar France was irresistible and the stamp of approval had been given without much thought of the difficulties.

Napier sighed and wondered if he would have voted for the operation if he'd been at the conference table.

Probably would have, he guessed. It was a time of wild schemes and far chances. Napier had come into intelligence after the war when things were a bit more reasoned and cautious.

The SOE in 1944 had burrowed into the files, working night and day to find their ideal target. It took time. When they finally focused on one candidate he wasn't in the Pas de Calais area or Brittany or Normandy as they had hoped but in the South. Napier could imagine the debates and arguments. He could also imagine the rationalization of their final decision. A Frenchman from the South was more Latin . . . ergo, more corruptible. He smiled to himself, guessing he wasn't far off the mark.

Operation Red Gold had been highly classified and restricted to a very small circle of officials on a need-to-know basis. The Prime Minister had been grumpily acquiescent and too busy with Eisenhower, De Gaulle and the coming invasion to spend much time on the plan. He'd made it clear from the start, poking his cigar at the SOE wizards that any mishap or revelation of the operation would bring a vigorous denial of involvement on the part of his government. The note on the Prime Minister's attitude toward Red Gold had been added to the dossier following his death in 1965. Napier guessed that whoever had done it was probably himself now under the sod.

So the wheels were put in motion. A very small section of SOE went to work on photographic blowups of a Michelin scale map with Château-Grignac in its upper right-hand corner and a growing file on one Beaulieu, Jean, local commander of the FTP.

They'd been lucky. Once contacted, Beaulieu had been receptive. Flattered and courted by an SOE agent during a meeting near Lyon, the young Beaulieu had been told that London judged his *maquis* highly effective . . . a model organization. He'd been promised special treatment. An extra drop of explosives, a delivery of medical supplies and a canister of new Sten guns had convinced him the British could be trusted.

At a follow-up rendezvous two months later the same SOE agent played on Beaulieu's vanity, ambition and greed. When Beaulieu left for Provence the next morning in an overloaded gasogene truck he wore a canvas belt stuffed with SOE money for his "emergency fund."

The web was woven skillfully around Beaulieu. A bit more money offered and accepted, more links with the SOE, more distance from party ideals and control. At one meeting his SOE contact produced secret documents detailing corruption among the Communist leaders of another FTP group. They were clever forgeries but they convinced Beaulieu that other comrades were feathering their own nests while fighting the war.

Finally, the *coup de grâce*. Beaulieu was offered a generous sum in return for a promise of continued cooperation with SOE. His British contact, by now almost a friend, had foreseen Beaulieu's possible objections and was ready for them. No, he was not compromising his political beliefs. In fact, the payment would provide Beaulieu with the funds he needed for his planned political career. Continued support was promised if Beaulieu cooperated with British Intelligence after the war. The British agent had told him he himself had been a wild-eyed radical in public school. "You Communists," he'd said jokingly, "are conservative parsons compared to some of us."

Jean Beaulieu had agreed. London was overjoyed.

Their fish netted, they set about arranging the delivery of funds. It had to be in solid form: something acceptable to anyone and untraceable during the war; something unaffected by the fluctuations of paper currencies in the expected confusion and chaos of a postwar Europe.

A tired SOE accountant had found the solution. In 1940 a treasure trove of gold from the vaults of a Lille bank had been seized by a British Army intelligence unit and trucked to the beach at Dunkirk. The gold had left France on a British destroyer eighteen hours before the first German scouts reached the evacuation beaches. The French gold had been commandeered by His Majesty's government as a contingency fund for SOE.

The meticulous accountant had remembered the gold from Lille. Though most of the shipment was in the form of gold bars, there were also several cases of gold coins. The napoleons, small, easily exchangeable and eagerly sought after in a country where prominent families and peasants alike made a fetish of hoarding gold even in peacetime, were perfect for clandestine use.

Beaulieu was to use only a fraction of the shipment for his wartime needs. The bulk of the gold was to be left in a safe cache till the war's end. It was then to be placed in the vaults of the Banque de Provence et Londres, a London-owned bank used by British Intelligence prior to the war. Beaulieu could then convert the gold to currency or use it, depending on his needs, with no questions asked.

As SOE could not risk dropping the gold directly to Beaulieu in full sight of his Communist *maquis*, it was decided that Major McCallister and his Sergeant Whipple of the nearby Réseau Renard would be the know-nothing recipients. They would be under orders to bury the gold at a prearranged location signaled to Beaulieu.

Strange, Napier thought, after all that trouble Beaulieu never did get his hands on the gold.

They'd told Napier in London that the current worth of the missing gold, allowing for market fluctuations, collectors prices and lot purity, was close to £600,000. That is, if it was still intact, not melted down or hidden under a hundred French mattresses. He put down his pipe. The summer heat was making him drowsy. What a business, he mused. MI6 hears of McCallister's return to France, asks him to do some snooping and the poor clod is dropped like a slow partridge. Probably without knowing why.

There was a tap on the door. Napier opened one of the insurance files, hid the gin bottle in a waste basket and placed some papers on the desk. He walked to the door and opened it. The Consul General's secretary smiled, showing some gold-capped teeth and offered him tea. He accepted a cup. As he was being served the secretary looked quickly around the office. He thanked her, put the cup down on the desk and locked the door. It was a good thing he'd changed the safe's combination. Curiosity and suspicion, he supposed, could be diplomatic assets.

CHAPTER V

JoJo le Lièvre was disappointed. He'd trawled the water-front bars and cafés for two days. The catch had been meager. His search for information on Lucien Brannec, the murdered commando, had produced nothing. But JoJo had a dogged quality, a sixth sense that told him there was a tie between Brannec's murder and that of the Englishman. Somehow, once he found it, he knew he'd profit from the discovery. JoJo was on his way to lunch in the Panier district, his fat legs rubbing together painfully as he puffed along the Rue du Refuge past dog droppings and scatterings of broken glass. He paused to catch his breath. A mangy mongrel growled at him from a nearby doorway. It was Friday and he always had a lunch of *couscous* on Friday at L'Étoile du Sud, a small Algerian restaurant in a narrow cobblestoned alley off the Rue du Refuge.

He resumed his progress and the dog, emboldened by his departure, ventured a threatening bark. JoJo ignored it. He was thinking of his next move. He knew Lucien Brannec had been linked with the underworld; the problem was to discover what part of the underworld. Marseille was like no other city in France. There was the underworld of the traditional gangster families; the underworld of the Union Corse; the underworld of the comparative newcomers, the North Africans and the black Africans; the underworld of the outsiders, the gangs from Nice and Lyon who kept small power bases in the city but infiltrated in force only for a big operation. It had been much simpler before. Everything had been neatly compartmentalized. There had been a certain discipline. Now there was a growing anarchy undermining the old order. The young were using violence when persuasion would have achieved the same results. They were undisciplined. They refused to take orders and they often laughed in the faces of the traditional *caïds* who had kept gangland relations finely balanced and mutually profitable.

JoJo turned into the alley and paused to wipe the perspiration from his brow. He could see the sign of L'Étoile du Sud now and he licked his lips in anticipation. He walked carefully over the uneven cobblestones and pushed open the restaurant's door. The automatic bell jangled, announcing his entry. Ahmed, the proprietor, greeted him with a wave from the small kitchen to the rear of the narrow room. Arab music was blaring from a battered transistor on the bar and most of the tables were full. The air was heavy with the odor of grilled *merguez*, fresh coriander and cumin. JoJo moved down the aisle, found himself a seat at a table with two other customers and picked up a grease stained menu. His Algerian tablemates were bent over steaming bowls of *chorba* spooning up the rich broth and picking the meat off the chicken bones.

The proprietor's wife, a grim faced Kabyle woman with a blue tattoo on her forehead, came to the table to take JoJo's order. He asked for the special *couscous* and a bottle of red Mascara. She put a small dish of hot *harrisa* sauce on the table and shuffled off to place his order in the kitchen. JoJo perused the dessert offerings on the menu and decided he'd have one of the honey-soaked Arab pastries later with his coffee. He examined the other tables. Most of the customers were North Africans but there was an elderly Frenchman sitting near the kitchen. An old colonial from the look of him. All in all, it was a group that JoJo found of little interest. He examined a flyspecked print of the Casbah hanging on the wall near his table and watched the proprietor's cat eating some food fragments from the linoleum floor.

When his heaping plate of *couscous* arrived he spooned the sauce over the hand-rolled semolina, dotted it with *harrisa* and filled his mouth with a *merguez*. Chewing the spicy sausage he thought again of Lucien Brannec. JoJo thought best when he was eating. By the time he'd finished half the *couscous* he'd decided on his next exploratory move. He would have to go further than Marseille. He'd begin by checking with some of his contacts in Toulon and work back up along the coast, stopping in Bandol where he'd first met Brannec. He drank a glass of the heavy Mascara, cut a large piece of mutton and speared it with his fork. The doorbell jangled behind him as more customers entered. While he was in Toulon he could do some other business. Joseph Cantini needed some information about an outsider, one Babu Amer, who was running prostitutes from Abidjan to Toulon, cutting into Cantini's Marseille-based enterprise.

By the time JoJo had finished his *couscous* and ordered dessert the restaurant was almost empty. As he savored the sticky pastry and sipped his thick, black coffee the doorbell heralded more departures. Only the latecomers who had taken seats near the door were still there. JoJo wiped his mouth with a napkin and prepared to pay his bill. The music was still blaring its discordant rhythm but the kitchen was strangely quiet. He called the proprietor's name. There was no answer. Frowning, he looked around for the man's wife. She was nowhere in sight. Even the cat had deserted the room. JoJo frowned, cursing under his breath. He was counting out the exact change to cover his meal when the two customers by the door rose quietly from their chairs. One of them, a tall young black man with curly hair, slid into the seat across from JoJo.

"Bonjour, JoJo," he said smiling. "Did you enjoy your *couscous?"*

JoJo's small eyes narrowed.

"Monsieur Amer sends his early condolences," the young man told him, the smile still etched on his face.

JoJo's chubby right hand moved slowly toward the folded straight razor in his hip pocket. The man behind him lunged forward driving the sharp blade of a thin knife deftly into the base of JoJo's neck, severing his spinal cord. JoJo jerked like a sledged bull and fell forward onto the table. The young black man who had spoken went through his pockets, examined their contents and replaced everything after carefully wiping his fingerprints off the wallet.

"Let's go," he told his companion, moving toward the door.

The assassin grabbed a handful of JoJo's hair in his left hand and jerked his head back off the table, exposing the fatty folds of his neck. In one quick movement he reached under JoJo's chin and slit his throat from ear to ear. A torrent of scarlet blood poured over the table. The killer wiped his knife on a napkin and replaced it under his coat in a shoulder sheath.

"Now," he said as they left the restaurant, "he smiles with two mouths."

Roger Bastide's steady breast stroke brought him to the end of the white-tile pool. He grabbed the iron ladder and shook the water from his head. Six laps were enough. He pulled himself out of the water, his heart thumping, and began to towel himself. He had needed the swim. He felt clearheaded and alive. He had time now for a light lunch in the sun before returning to the office.

The restaurant of the Cercle Sportif de Marseille was already crowded with members passing through the cafeteria line and sitting at the Formica-topped tables devouring their *steak-frites* and shredded-carrot salads. Children were dripping melting ice cream sticks on the floor and some bronzed teenagers were laughing and flirting at a corner table. Bastide had joined the Cercle for the swimming alone. He found the young children noisy, the teenagers spoiled and brash and the adults a strange mix of earnest sportsmen and couples involved in intricate sex relationships. He couldn't really blame them. A glance in any direction proved what a minimum of bathing suit could do for a maximum of well-rounded female flesh. He moved with the line, tray in hand, ordered a grilled *entrecôte-salade* and served himself a small carafe of rosé. He nodded a greeting to a forty-year-old widow with the svelte, tanned figure of a twenty-year-old.

She was having an affair with the husband of her best friend, and when the husband was away on business she was often the organizer of *partouze* orgies in her apartment. Leland of the Vice Squad had told Bastide he had Polaroid photos in his safe of the widow's parties mailed to him anonymously by some disgruntled participant. The widow, Leland explained, featured in every print as the centerpiece of varied multisex entanglements. He watched the widow's well-formed *derrière* sway as she carried her tray to a table and wondered how many respectable members of the Cercle, male or female, had sampled her charms. He sighed and decided to think of other things.

His steak came sizzling from the kitchen and he found a table on the terrace. He had just cut into his meat when a shadow blocked the sun.

Mireille Perraud smiled down at him, mischievously. "Well, *monsieur l'inspecteur,* do you often eat alone?"

He wiped his mouth, stood up and they exchanged the ritual kiss on each cheek.

"And you?" Bastide asked. "Would you care to join me?"

"No, thank you. I am with friends . . . over there." She gestured to a table by the terrace railing. "I will have a glass of wine with you."

Bastide left Mireille to get a clean wine glass from a tray on the bar. He returned and poured her some rosé. She was wearing a white bikini and the effect was even more stunning than when he had last seen her. She tapped a cigarette out of a packet and lit it with a small golden lighter. When she bent over to put the lighter back in her straw bag the untanned swell of her firm breasts appeared over the thin strip of bikini bra.

"Your steak will get cold," Mireille warned, aware of his interest.

He dropped his eyes to his plate and speared a piece of rare beef with his fork. "How is your husband?" Bastide asked, filling his mouth.

"He will be back in two weeks," she told him. "His ship is in America. Norfolk, Virginia." She picked up her wine, her blue eyes watching him over the glass. "Why don't you call me sometime? I come over here at least once a week. You could invite me to lunch."

He laughed. "A policeman doesn't have much time for leisurely luncheons with beautiful women," he said. "And a short lunch with a beautiful woman is worse than none."

She rubbed her thighs. They glistened with suntan oil. "Toulon can be very boring," she said. "Bridge with the Navy wives and charitable projects don't interest me. I sit in Toulon, listen to the bugle calls and watch my hips grow."

"You have no worries there," Bastide commented.

He was beginning to wish he hadn't come to the Cercle for lunch. He'd lost interest in his steak, in the sun, in any thought of the McCallister case. All that concerned him at the moment was Mireille. It wasn't a tender preoccupation or memories of their teenage infatuation. It was a crotch-tightening, throbbing desire to make love to her; to caress and kiss her breasts; to thrust his hand between her legs; to carry her off to a bed and take her once and for all.

She lifted one foot onto the chair and peeled some sunburned skin off her knee. Her position was provocative, accentuating her sex and the linear purity of her long legs.

"Why are you frowning?" she asked innocently.

He hadn't realized he'd been so obvious. "Just thinking," he mumbled, finishing his wine. What was left of his steak was completely cold. He pushed it aside along with the salad. Despite the wine his throat felt dry and he knew he would be in a bad mood the rest of the afternoon. He would have done better to eat at La Mère Pascal.

Bastide's office was crowded when he returned. Inspector Mattei was looking at a city map and two other detectives were telephoning.

Bastide frowned. "What's up?" he asked.

"JoJo le Lièvre." Mattei made a throat-slitting motion. "Bled like a pig."

Bastide took off his coat and threw it over the chair behind his desk.

"He was helping us find information on the McCallister affair," Mattei said. "It looks as if he did."

"Where?"

"Some Algerian *gargote* up in the Panier. Died at his favorite pastime . . . eating."

"Any leads?"

"I've got the owner outside. Just about to talk to him. Shall I bring him in?"

Bastide nodded and sat down.

Ahmed Bouchara was a small, thin man with a heavy head of dark hair and long sideburns. He had the eyes of a frightened fawn as he entered the office, looking quickly from one policeman to the other.

"Sit down," Mattei ordered, pointing to an empty chair.

Bouchara did as he was told. Bastide noticed the man's hands were shaking.

"You're the proprietor of L'Étoile du Sud?" Mattei asked.

Bouchara nodded. *"Oui,* monsieur."

"I didn't hear you!" Mattei snapped.

"*Oui*, monsieur," Bouchara repeated.

Mattei proceeded with the questioning. He covered JoJo le Lièvre's visits to the restaurant, the people he'd talked with and conversations he'd had with Bouchara. Then he asked Bouchara to detail what had happened prior to JoJo's murder. The Algerian hesitated, trying to select a verbal path that would satisfy the police and not antagonize those responsible for JoJo's death. But it was difficult and Mattei had been too long in the trade to grant him reflection time.

"One man told my wife he wanted us to leave the restaurant."

"When?"

"He told her to bring their first course, wait till the other occupied tables were free. Then we were to leave by the back door."

"So you just left? Is this normal? Someone tells you to leave your own restaurant and you obey?"

Bouchara's mouth worked nervously. He glanced at Bastide, but Bastide's face was a mask, showing nothing.

"Well?" Mattei demanded. "I'm waiting."

Bouchara shifted his eyes to the floor. "You know how it is in the Panier," he said.

"No, I don't. You tell me."

"It's . . . it is very difficult. There are bad people sometimes. A dangerous place. I want no trouble. My wife and I, we are cautious. I saw these men. I knew we should go when they told us to leave."

"Why?"

Bouchara swallowed. He spread his hands and raised his brown eyes to look at Mattei.

"They were bad men."

"How did you know?"

"The look of them. They . . . were tough ones, *les durs*. Not just *voyous*."

"You mean professionals?"

Bouchara nodded. "Yes, that is it . . . professionals."

"Murderers?"

The word seemed to send a shock through Bouchara's thin body. "I did not say that," he mumbled.

"You said they were professionals. Professional what? Professional yachtsmen? Professional engineers? Professional pimps?"

Bouchara was silent. He wiped his forehead with the palm of his hand.

"Look, Monsieur Bouchara," Mattei told him, sitting down on the edge of Bastide's desk. "A man was murdered in your flytrap. If you had not taken orders from his killers, he might still be alive. Perhaps it was all planned. Were you working with them?"

"I didn't know them," Bouchara pleaded. "I'd never seen them before today."

"As you wish." Mattei gestured to a detective who had just finished telephoning. "Take him along for a full deposition and make sure you get a thorough description of the two heavies. Where's his wife?"

"She's outside," the detective told him. "Wailing like a deserted bride."

"Well, I'll talk to her later. Keep them apart."

The detective took Bouchara's arm. "*Allez, en route!*" he said, lifting the Algerian off his chair.

Mattei sighed. "What do you think?" he asked Bastide.

"I think he's probably telling the truth. Has he had any other trouble? How about his own record?"

"Clean enough. Works hard. Has four kids. Smokes a little hashish. What's your guess?"

Mattei folded his hairy arms. "JoJo had enemies, no doubt about that. But he was a useful man to a lot of people. A mine of information. Sort of a neutral source. He'd developed an operational technique that stopped short of ordinary informing. He always held back a bit, didn't often step over the line."

Bastide picked up a pencil and tapped it on his chin. "You think this was the McCallister case?"

"He was trying to follow up on the killer. I told him I wanted a check on information or rumors pointing to a professional coming in from the outside. Above all, he was looking for links with our local gangs."

"He may have found one."

Mattei nodded. "Found it and lost it at the same time."

"I think . . ." Bastide's phone rang. He answered it. It was *Sous*-Inspecteur Guichard of the Police Judiciare in Toulon. "I might have something of interest," he told Bastide. "It's on that garroting the other day."

Bastide searched his mind, trying to remember the details. "Oh," he replied, "that. Look, I'm tied up with something very important. Can't you talk to the man who's handling the case. I'll have you transferred . . ."

"This, I think, is important."

Bastide made a face in Mattei's direction. "Very well. Go ahead."

"I've been checking the Naval records at the Arsenal. A routine measure at the request of your office in regard to the corpse fished out of the sea. You know, the tattooed man?"

"Yes?"

"I think I've found him. Brannec, Lucien. The description fits. So do the fingerprints. I'm waiting for a dental report but I'm sure it was Brannec. Dishonorably dis-

charged from the Marine Commandos five years
ago . . ."

Bastide interrupted Guichard. "*Bon sang*, Guichard!"
he snapped, "I told you I'm not handling that one personally. I'm up to my ass in something else!"

"Hold it!" Guichard pleaded. "Listen to this. Brannec
was an expert rifleman. A sharpshooter. His commando
specialty is listed in his service record. He was a sniper."

"Are you sure?"

"Positive. I thought this would be of interest, considering the McCallister murder."

Bastide smiled. "You're a genius, Guichard. Good
work. Now, take it from there. Try to trace his path after
the discharge. We'll start digging too. Put some copies of
that service record on the wire to us and to Paris. Does
the Navy have any mug shots?"

"Yes. I've got one right here, stapled to his record."

"Good. We'll need copies. Check any addresses he
might have given, try to see if he had any friends still in
the service or in Toulon."

Mattei, sensing Bastide's elation, was leaning over the
desk.

"Oh, and Guichard," Bastide continued, "put a
stakeout on the villa of Colonel Lebrun. Yes. License
plates, visitors, the usual. No, I don't have anything
solid. Good. Call me tomorrow evening." He put down
the telephone.

"*Alors?*" Mattei asked eagerly.

"Babar, it seems our dead commando was a sharpshooter, trained as a sniper."

"The man on the ridge!"

"Maybe. At least it fits. Someone doesn't believe in
loose ends."

The afternoon sun filtered through the leaves of the old olive tree throwing a dappled pattern of light and shadow on the table. The hum of slow-moving honey bees and the constant buzzing of cicadas formed a soft counterpoint to the drums and sudden trumpets of the military music playing on the small cassette machine. Colonel Lebrun held the small figurine at arm's length, turning it slowly. He was repainting some of the soldiers of his collection. He held a model of a mounted spahi brandishing a saber. The table was cluttered with small paintpots, brushes and cleaning rags. A reference book on military uniforms was open before him and he glanced at a color illustration, comparing it with his handiwork.

"The cape is passable," he commented, "but I don't like the beard. He looks like a Jew, not a Muslim!"

His guest pushed his spotless panama back from his forehead and peered at the model. "*Mon colonel,* you are right. He looks like a mad rabbi."

The colonel grunted and plunged his brush into the cleaning fluid. He wiped his bony hands on a rag. "Another drink, Pignon?"

"No, not in this heat," Gabriel Pignon replied, listening to the majestic rhythms of the "Marche Impériale" with his eyes closed.

Pignon was the colonel's friend, a retired major of the Colonial Infantry. He was considerably younger than the colonel. The colonel picked up a *sapeur* of the Legion, eyeing the model critically. The ax was correct but the leather apron was too yellow.

"The policeman has not come again?" Pignon asked, his eyes still shut.

"No, I have not been bothered. I gave him lunch when he came. A dull fellow. I know a bit about him. He was a *para* during the Algerian war."

"Undisciplined crowd."

"Worse than that. He was one of those bleeding hearts who objected to getting rough with the fellagha. Questioned orders and lost his sergeant's stripes."

"What do you think he's after?"

"He's looking for a scapegoat! I told him it was probably the English . . . one of their SIS operations."

"Do you honestly believe that?"

"No," the colonel grinned, "not at all. Too dramatic for an English operation. They would have done away with McCallister quietly, with no fuss. In any case, I enjoy playing the muddled, old militarist."

"Has he been bothering your people?"

"Oh, he's questioned those he could find. But I am not concerned."

"You can trust them?"

"Of course, Pignon, of course. The war is over but they still march to my command."

"Well, this inspector, he doesn't seem to be making great progress."

"What do you expect. The poor fellow. He is in a hot pan. The government breathing down his neck; the British involved; the Socialist Party watching like hawks; the Communists aggressive and suspicious . . ."

"Not to mention you."

"I will not interfere. *If* the investigation is properly done and the findings make sense. We have nothing to hide. On the other hand, if any of those pseudorevolutionaries in the government try to involve us . . . they will regret it." The colonel paused, squinting up at the sun. "They have no idea how strong we are. The Right in France—the true Right—is a powerful force. Like a fist, ready to strike. Let them beware!"

"Come now, *mon colonel,* one must not exaggerate."

"I'm not. You should see the young ones who come to see me. Clean, straightforward, determined. The hope of a new France. You, Pignon, should be more involved. It is exhilarating."

"I prefer to draw my pension and sit at a café on the Quai Stalingrad watching the pretty girls go by."

The colonel frowned at his friend. "That is another thing. We must have that name changed. One of the finest promenades in our city named for a Bolshevik defeat!"

"I thought it was a victory."

"Bah, propaganda. The Germans smashed Stalingrad to rubble. I've written to the City Council about it. A disgrace."

Roger Bastide climbed the worn stone stairs to his apartment. He was tired and needed a shower; his summer suit was wrinkled. It had been a day full of frustrations. The only bright spot had been Guichard's news from Toulon on Lucien Brannec. It was too early to call it a breakthrough or hope for the best. He always expected the worst. Anything better was pure gravy. But he couldn't concentrate on his work. His mind kept returning to Mireille Perraud as he had seen her at the Cercle. She'd said she was bored in Toulon. Was that a hint, a signal? He searched for his key and it crossed his mind that an official trip to Toulon might be in order. Guichard didn't know the details of the case and something might slip by him. He unlocked the door to his apartment and smiled. Bastide, he told himself, you are fooling no one. If you want to go to Toulon—go!

"Bonjour!" Janine Bourdet called to him from the balcony. She was sprawled on one of his deck chairs, topless under the sun, two wads of damp cotton protecting her eyes. "It is *you,* isn't it?" she asked.

"Yes, it's me," Bastide replied. "But what if it hadn't been? It could have been a mad rapist."

"I prefer a sane lover."

He threw his jacket over a chair and walked over to stand by her. Even in repose Janine's body radiated a lubricity, an erotic appeal that most women could never achieve. Bastide squatted beside the deck chair and ran one hand over her rounded hip, into her small waist and up to her right breast. He cupped her breast, lifting it slightly and ran his thumb lightly over the nipple.

Janine removed the cotton from one eye and peered at him quizzically. *"Oh là là!"* she commented. *"Monsieur l'inspecteur* is incorrigible."

He closed her mouth with his lips, kissing her deeply and hard, pulling her to him with his left arm behind her shoulders. She tried to disentangle herself but he held her tightly. "But . . ." she began.

"Don't move," he told her, running his lips along her throat, breathing the odor of her perfume.

"Be sensible, Roger," she pleaded. "Not here."

"We have only the police helicopters to worry about," he told her, slipping off his trousers and throwing his shirt after them. "And they are busy elsewhere."

"But this chair," she reasoned, tossing aside the other cotton pad and untying her bikini bottom, "it won't support . . ."

He kissed her again. She ran her hand over his shoulders and into the hair at the nape of his neck. He pulled away slightly after a moment and looked into her eyes. They had the soft look of readiness. He reached behind him, took the cushion off the other deck chair and dropped it onto the floor of the balcony. With a quick movement he lifted her free of the chair and put her gently on the cushion.

"Salaud!" she said, kissing him again, her knees rising high, her practiced hand reaching for him. "This is not comfortable."

"Maybe," he murmured, entering her slowly, "but it is good."

They took their time in a ritual of sharing sensations and accepting pleasure. It was especially voluptuous with the sun tingling on his back and the smell of the sea around them. Her body was warm, tightening with the sudden urgency they shared, writhing to meet him. Her eyes closed now, her head went back, arching her neck. He drove hard as they breathed as one. Her abrupt cry was lost amid the squawking of gulls wheeling overhead. Bastide supported himself on his elbows, smiling down at her. She opened her eyes and they kissed briefly, smiling.

"I liked that," he told her huskily.

"I hadn't planned to," she said, "but so did I."

"I think my knee's bleeding a bit," he remarked, glancing down at his right leg.

"You deserve it." She ran her long fingers up and down his ribs. She was suddenly serious. "This may have to stop one of these days."

"Stop?"

"Yes. Monsieur Gautier allows me a certain freedom

but I'm sure he knows about us. If it becomes an embarrassment, he'll order me not to see you again."

He frowned at her. "For God's sake, let's not ruin
everything."

She smiled again, shaking her head. "And you call
yourself a realist!"

He rolled to one side, leaned over and kissed a still
taut nipple.

"Oh, no," she cautioned, pushing him away and sitting
up. "I came here to profit from your balcony in peace.
Now the sun is almost gone."

He watched her leave the balcony, walking lightly on
her toes, her firm buttocks jiggling slightly. He sighed
and lay back on the mat with his hands behind his head,
staring at the blue sky. He should have been satisfied and
content. It irritated him that he wasn't. The image of
Mireille hung in his mind. Until he made a special effort
to erase it, he imagined what it would have been like if
Mireille had been waiting for him on the balcony.

They ate dinner at La Mère Pascal. It was a slow night
and Dominique came to sit with them when she finished
cooking. Her husband insisted on offering them green
Izarra with their coffee. Bastide had eaten lightly as he
planned to visit his mother in Arles the next morning.
Janine had made up for his abstemiousness with a *salade
niçoise* and *rognons de veau provençale*. He had settled for a
rare *filet*.

"Tell your mother I am still waiting for the recipes she
promised me," Dominique said, her bare arms dark
against the white tablecloth. "The cuisine of Arles is fine
art and she is a true *arlésienne.* " Bastide agreed, knowing
that he could count on two hours or more at his mother's
table the next day.

Dominique and Janine launched into an interminable conversation on the pitfalls of three-star restaurants in Paris. Bastide sipped his Izarra and thought about the deaths of JoJo le Lièvre and Lucien Brannec. He had passed by Commissaire Aynard's office to tell him about Brannec, but Aynard had been home nursing his ulcer. It was just as well. Bastide wasn't ready to listen to Aynard's deductions and suggestions. Bastide knew he shouldn't go to Arles in the morning. There was too much work to do. But he would leave early and get back after lunch. Mattei could hold the fort. He knew there was a limit to the time he could go without seeing his mother. He was well past it already.

They walked back to his apartment slowly, pausing to watch the well-dressed theater goers leaving the Théâtre de la Criée on the Quai de Rive Neuve.

"You know, Roger," Janine said, "perhaps someday I will buy a restaurant."

He looked at her surprised. "You?"

"What's so unusual about that? You expect me to train courtesans?"

"I didn't say that. I just don't see you in the restaurant business."

They reached his apartment house and he took her arm. *"Allez,"* he said, starting up the stairs, "to the summit!"

"Doucement," she laughed, "we've been there once already today."

Bastide left Marseille in a police sedan before eight. He took the autoroute to Salon and struck off to the left over the plain. The low peaks of the Alpilles were soon in sight and he found himself whistling an Aznavour tune as he passed slow-moving trucks and air-conditioned tourist buses. He stopped in Arles and bought a bouquet of chrysanthemums and a bottle of port. He crossed the Rhone and within fifteen minutes turned into a small road shaded by a stand of bamboo. He crossed a stone bridge and slowed as the road became a dirt track leading to his mother's house. The house was an old, thick-walled farm with shuttered windows and a tile roof. Two leafy plane trees shaded the stone flagging of a front terrace surrounded by rose bushes.

He pulled to a stop. An aging retriever shuffled out of the open front door, his tail wagging. Then she was there in the sunlight, a hand on each hip and her gray head nodding as he climbed from the car.

"*Eh ba!* It's not possible. You've finally come."

He took her in his arms, kissing her on both cheeks. "You're younger than ever," he said, looking at her. "Been chasing Monsieur Fontet again?"

"That old fool," she replied. "He is too old for me."

Bastide had that familiar wrenching of the heart as he contemplated his mother. One of these days soon she'd be gone and he couldn't do anything about it. He knew he'd miss her. He also knew he wasn't doing enough for her. She had the fine bones of a handsome woman. Her brown skin was crosshatched with a thousand tiny wrinkles and stray wisps of gray hair had escaped from the bun on the back of her head. Holding her hands he could feel the hardness of the calluses and he felt a sudden, deep sadness, remembering their soft touch when he'd been young.

"Come, *mon petit*," she ordered jocularly, as if she'd deciphered his train of thought, "in out of this heat." She

led the way into the cool interior and he could smell the
rich fragrance from her country kitchen.

"I've brought you some flowers," he said, "and a bottle of port for an apéritif."

She shrugged. "I have all the flowers I need in the
garden. You shouldn't have wasted your money." It was
the same ritual at each visit, but she would have been
disappointed if he hadn't brought gifts.

"The port I shall save for the winter," she said. This
too was a tradition. She always emptied the bottle between visits. He braced himself for the next question.
"Still not married?"

"Of course not," he laughed.

She sighed and sat down on a sagging divan. "Come
sit next to me and tell me about your work."

He made the attempt but she really wasn't interested.
He was able to direct the conversation to the local gossip
and her garden. She told him of the apricots and how
sweet they were but said the peaches were smaller this
year. She complained about a Gypsy family that had stolen one of her chickens, but he did not take this too
seriously as the same incident was recounted every year,
slightly altered or more dramatically emphasized. He
wondered how soon she would get around to the church.
He didn't have long to wait. She started with the miracle
that had saved his uncle Marius from drowning in the
Camargue and how Marius had become a regular
churchgoer after that. Then she looked at him sideways
to suggest that God should have a place "in your business."

This was his cue to go in search of some pastis in the
kitchen. "They say God is everywhere," he said over his

shoulder as he poured himself a drink and selected a glass for his mother's port.

"He is, *petit,* but he can't reach people who won't listen."

The sight of the glasses took her mind off God. "Ah, wait till I get you something to chew on. That *anis* will rot your stomach if you don't coat it first." He smiled after her, watching her move over the tiled floor. He glanced around the room. It was neat and clean, each piece of furniture in place as he always remembered it. He walked to a framed photograph hanging on the wall. A younger Roger Bastide stared back at him, a *para* beret cocked over one eye, husky bare arms folded under the turned-up sleeves of a large pocketed parachute jacket. Behind him the dark, jagged line of the Aurès Mountains. How long ago? Another man, another life.

"Here," his mother hurried into the room carrying a battered metal tray with two small plates on it. "Your father's favorite . . . *olives picholines!*" Bastide nodded his approval, breathing in the odor of fennel, laurel, coriander and orange peel used in their preparation.

"They sell them ready-made now in Arles," she said with distaste, "but they don't use the old method, the damp wood cinders. That is what makes them!" Bastide helped himself to one of the tasty, pitless olives.

"And here are some almonds from Monsieur Fontet's trees. The best in the region."

They sat and talked of his brother and sister and then of his aunts and uncles. After she'd finished her port she suggested it was time he found a sensible occupation and settled down to raise a family. When they moved to the kitchen table for lunch she entered her period of reminiscences and he listened attentively knowing how happy she was to revisit the past. The lunch lived up to his expectations and he was glad he'd eaten sparingly the night before and at breakfast.

The first dish was a *salade de moules au safron;* the tender mussels were mixed with fine slices of potato and dressed in mayonnaise flavored with lemon juice and saffron. They drank a dry white wine from Les Baux and cleaned their plates with thick slices of *pain de campagne.*

Estouffade de boeuf arlésienne followed, served in an old casserole of faience. The rich beef stew, redolent of herbs, garlic and reduced white wine, spotted with black olives and crowned with finely chopped parsley, was one of Bastide's favorite dishes. His mother presented the casserole as if she were serving royalty. As he filled their plates she returned to the kitchen for a plate of fresh green beans sautéed in a dash of olive oil. She put them on the table and ground black pepper over them.

"Today we will drink some of your father's Châteauneuf-du-Pape," she announced, plucking an already opened bottle from the elaborate Provençal sideboard.

"You should save it," Bastide protested.

"For what?" she asked. "Your marriage?"

CHAPTER VI

The jukebox was silent in the Café des Colonies. It wasn't exactly a wake, but there was little conversation. JoJo le Lièvre's sudden death had affected everyone there in varying degrees. None of the other regulars had liked JoJo but the fact of his permanent absence reminded them of their own mortality. They sipped their drinks in silence, reflecting on their recent activities, wondering if any of their actions, contacts or unguarded comments could possibly produce the same, fatal, result. The *patron* leaned his bulk on the bar and chewed on a toothpick.

"He could eat," he said, reflectively. "I'll say that for him."

Ramon Souche grunted in agreement. Bouche d'Or sighed and Georges Astier said nothing. A warm breeze moved the beaded yellow curtain over the door and blew some dust onto the floor.

"He loved pasta," the *patron* continued. "I've seen him eat a full plate of cannelloni, follow it with spaghetti and finish off with ravioli." He shook his head, picked up a cloth and began to wipe a glass. No one mentioned the murder, the circumstances or who might have done it. They had their own ideas but such conjecture lay outside the etiquette of the Café des Colonies.

Mattei's abrupt arrival broke the silence. He pushed

aside the beads and paused just inside the door. The *patron* frowned at him and the others looked quickly away, turning their backs. Mattei walked to the bar.

"A sad thing," he said. "Poor JoJo. A very cool pastis, *patron*."

He waited as the drink was served. Then he turned to look out the door. "Don't despair. We're on the case. We'll do our best. That's why I'm here. I asked myself, Who can help? It was obvious. JoJo's friends."

Bouche d'Or snorted in derision. Mattei chose to ignore him.

"So, here I am," Mattei continued, "ready to listen." He swung back to the bar and clamped his huge hand on Souche's shoulder. "Anything to tell me, Ramon?"

Souche stiffened. "I know nothing," he replied, glancing at the others.

"And you, Georges?" Mattei asked, addressing Astier, Souche still in his grip.

Astier shook his head. Mattei turned to Bouche d'Or. "How about the flesh trader? Surely you have some information that would bring a killer to justice?"

Bouche d'Or spread his hands and raised his shoulder. "Nothing," he replied. "Absolutely nothing."

Mattei pretended to be shocked. He released Souche, leaned over the bar and grabbed the *patron's* biceps. "It's unbelievable, *patron!* JoJo's best friends . . . and they know nothing. Surely you can help?"

The *patron's* pudgy face wrinkled with distaste. He nodded his head toward Mattei's hand. "Let go of me," he demanded.

"Oh," Mattei playacted, "I'm sorry. It must be the emotion I feel." He relaxed his grip. Mattei sighed and drank his pastis. He was now bored with the charade.

"Very well," he told them, "I've had enough of this shit. It's time for private conversations now. I'll expect all of you at my office tomorrow starting at ten in the morning. Understood?"

"I've got no replacement," the *patron* said. "I've got to open the bar."

"Close it," Mattei suggested.

"But . . ."

"Better yet," Mattei interrupted, "I'll send a food inspector up to look at that roach breeder you call a kitchen. Then you won't have to open for a few months."

He turned to the others. "Why don't you all come down together? You could share a taxi." He paid for his pastis and walked to the door. "Tomorrow at ten. Be prompt. I wouldn't like to come looking for you. It would put me off schedule and you'd have to spend the night as my guests."

Mattei walked along the cracked sidewalk to his Mercedes. As he bent over to unlock the door a stone whizzed by his head and slammed into a nearby wall. He swung around in time to see two young boys disappear behind a deserted building. There was no use chasing them. They had too much of a head start.

The man appeared suddenly on the narrow path. Député-Maire Jean Beaulieu started involuntarily. His springer spaniel barked and backed away from the intruder, growling. Beaulieu called him to heel but kept a wary eye on the stranger and tightened his grip on his walking stick.

"I'm sorry to have surprised you," the man said, smiling.

Beaulieu sized him up quickly: the mustache, white

eyebrows, the cut of his clothes, the florid complexion. An Englishman, Beaulieu told himself. No doubt about it. The pine wood around them was silent except for the far-off cry of a jay. The afternoon sun was filtering through the trees, turning the nearby cliffs ocher.

"Can I help you?" Beaulieu asked, relaxing.

"I'm afraid I'm a bit lost," Colin Napier responded. "I'm on my way to Château-Grignac."

Beaulieu smiled. "So am I." He gestured with his stick. "It's in this direction. I'll show you the way."

"That's kind of you," Napier said, falling in beside Beaulieu.

They had taken only a few steps before Napier paused and cleared his throat. Beaulieu stopped, puzzled. His spaniel growled again.

"Monsieur le député-maire," Napier said quietly, "I do not want to cause you any trouble. The war is over and much has been forgotten."

Beaulieu felt a coldness along his spine. He blinked at Napier, trying to remain calm. Napier sensed his uneasiness and spoke quickly.

"I've come out here so our meeting would be unobserved. London has no desire to dig up the past. But the unfortunate death of Ian McCallister has raised questions. If you cooperate I may never have to see you again."

Beaulieu swallowed, feeling the perspiration appearing on his forehead. "I don't understand," he said but his own words sounded hollow.

"I think you do. Let us finish this quickly, for your sake . . . and mine. Following the war all the circumstances of the drop intended for you were investigated. It was proven that you did not receive the gold. MI6 closed the

case; in fact, it was glad to do so as it had been a miserable failure . . ."

"Monsieur, you are wasting your time," Beaulieu
snapped, walking off along the path.

"Wait, please," Napier called after him in a firm voice.
"I know the background of Operation Red Gold . . . as
we called it."

Beaulieu came to a complete halt and turned slowly.
He was pale and distracted. Napier strode over to him.

"That is the last time I hope to mention it," he said.
"But I must now ask you to tell me who could have taken
the gold and who do you think murdered McCallister?"

Beaulieu rallied his strength. "Do you realize you are
talking to a member of the Assemblée Nationale? I don't
know who you are. Why should I answer any of your
questions?"

Napier frowned, pursing his lips. When he spoke his
voice had an acid bite. "One word from me, one leak to
the press about Operation Red Gold and your political
career, your life, would be ruined."

Beaulieu shifted his weight to the walking stick. He
looked down at the ground. Good shot, Napier thought,
I've winged him. It was not too bad a result considering
headquarters would never have allowed him to disclose
anything about Red Gold. He'd gambled on Beaulieu's
reaction and won.

"I'm waiting," Napier said, looking up and down the
path.

"Do you have any identification?" Beaulieu asked.

"Here," Napier replied, producing his official passport. "It's all you're going to see."

Beaulieu leafed through the passport and returned it.
"It tells me nothing."

"It's British and it's official. That should tell you something. Come now, neither of us can afford to be seen together and it's getting late. Please answer my questions."

"The gold," Beaulieu said hesitantly, "remains a mystery. It was not there when we arrived . . . but it had been. I found McCallister and one gold napoleon in the dirt. That is all. And thank God!"

Napier raised an eyebrow. It was not lost on Beaulieu.

"Yes, *monsieur l'anglais*. I said thank God . . . and I am a Communist. That should not surprise you. I presume you are supposed to be an expert on France. I was young and ambitious then. I was also tough and ruthless. I might have taken your gold. I might have betrayed my Party and my country."

Napier raised his hand. "With all respect, you are not on the floor of the Assemblée Nationale now."

"As to McCallister's death," Beaulieu continued, "that is a police matter. Of one thing you can be sure—it was not one of us."

"But you do have your suspicions?"

Beaulieu's paleness had given way to a blotched crimson. Anger was replacing his initial fear.

"Listen," he said, "if you harass me any further I shall call in the DST."

Napier smiled. "I don't think so." He pulled a leather-covered hip flask from his pocket. "I think we could use a drink, don't you?"

Beaulieu turned and strode off down the path, his impatient dog running on ahead of him.

Napier unscrewed the flask top and raised the flask to Beaulieu's retreating figure. "To all God-fearing Communists," he toasted, "wherever they may be."

The *député-maire's* mind was not on the meeting. The City Council of Château-Grignac were struggling with a sewage problem, but Jean Beaulieu was dealing with the implications of yesterday's meeting in the woods. The British must be mad sending someone to him now, after all these years. He remembered the Englishman's flat voice. "Who could have taken the gold? Who do you think murdered McCallister?" It was as if he'd asked, "Who's playing rugby in the Parc des Princes this weekend? Who is the captain of the French team?" As if the words had no special meaning. But they had meaning for him.

"Don't you agree?" One of the council members was addressing him directly, looking a bit perplexed at Beaulieu's unaccustomed lack of attention. Beaulieu fiddled with his spectacles and made a pretense of pondering the question. "I feel," the man continued, "we absolutely cannot proceed with the work without additional government funds."

"Are you sure?" Beaulieu asked, stalling for time.

"Well, you yourself said the street repairs took priority over the new sewer pipes."

"I did, I did," Beaulieu replied nodding. "What's your view, Dionne?" he asked addressing the town engineer.

"Well, considering the technical aspects of the pipe laying . . ."

Beaulieu's question had been a tactic. Dionne was a windbag. He'd devote a good ten minutes to any question that required a two-minute response. The *député-maire* pulled down his vest and made a show of sitting back to listen. His troubled mind returned to his prime problem. How far were the British likely to go? Perhaps this first meeting was the beginning of a campaign to discredit him? Who could have taken the gold? He wished he knew. There had been rumors of course. He'd had his suspicions. For some time after the war he'd watched the Socialist Hugo Paradisi. Paradisi's successful shipping venture seemed to have sprung from nowhere. Beaulieu had dug into Paradisi's business dealings with no tangible results. Paradisi's hands were soiled from lucrative postwar smuggling in the Mediterranean, but so were those of many "honorable" businessmen. In fact, it was Paradisi's wife who had brought her family money along to finance his shipping firm.

Then there was the colonel. Lebrun was definitely a madman, then and now. Beaulieu had always thought Lebrun belonged in an institution. He had the fine, dangerous cleverness of the insane. Beaulieu knew Lebrun was still revered by a group of right-wing fanatics in the Var and that he maintained contact with fascist student organizations in Aix and in Nice. But that didn't prove he'd taken the gold or make him a murderer.

Beaulieu glanced at the wall clock. The meeting must end in ten more minutes. His assistant, a bearded party member in a Lacoste shirt and expensive slacks, was already gathering up his papers and putting the cap on his pen.

". . . I therefore suggest," Dionne was winding up, "that we await the final report from the Bridge and Road Department before we vote on the sewage project."

Beaulieu glanced down the table. Every one seemed content with Dionne's suggestion. They were anxious to leave the stifling room and get home to their lunches. Normally he would have attacked Dionne's position and forced a vote. He hated to carry business over from one meeting to the next. But he had no stomach for it today.

He closed the session, shook hands with the departing council members and returned to his office. He shut the heavy oak doors, dropped his working file on his desk and walked to the open window to look out on the square. He could hear the click of *pétanque* balls and the wry comments of the players. A blackbird lit on the branch of a plane tree twenty feet away. It eyed him quizzically, turning its head as if waiting for him to speak. He hardly noticed it.

Was the Englishman working with the police? He'd have to find out. It would be delicate. If he asked the Party's help officially, there would be questions. He didn't want any more links with the McCallister case. He could explain the visit of the inspector and any further calls from the police by his known role in the local Resistance. Having someone investigate the Englishman would be another matter. It would have to be someone he could trust. He sighed, produced his pocket watch and flicked it open. It was time for lunch and he didn't feel like eating alone in his office. It was Thursday and the Café de la Poste's specialty was boeuf en Daube. No matter how grave the crisis, Jean Beaulieu always had a countryman's hearty appetite.

Commissaire Aynard was at his repulsive best. "The speed of your progress on this case," he told Roger Bastide, "would shame a snail. The Ministry called this morning. They are losing patience. Look at my desk . . . paperwork undone, unfinished reports. I'm too busy making excuses to Paris while you and Mattei scratch your asses and wonder where to look next. Let me tell you, Bastide, my patience is limited."

"It's a complicated case," Bastide replied slowly.

"Oh, it certainly is. A murder in broad daylight, plenty of witnesses, links with the war. I faced more difficult situations as a young detective in Lyon." Aynard shook his head and pulled at his ear lobe nervously. "Did you see the story in *Paris-Match?*" he asked. Bastide nodded.

"Yes," Aynard continued, "I'm sure you did. Everyone has, including the Minister. Very dramatic photos taken from the ridge at Roucas. The McCallister affair is developing into another Dominici case. The longer it drags on the worse it will get. I warn you, if you don't come up with something solid soon, I'll give it to someone else."

"We're working on the link with the Brannec murder. Lucien Brannec was a trained sharpshooter. He could have been the man on the ridge."

"I know, I know, I read your report." Aynard belched. "He was also a small-time criminal who could have been killed in some minor gang dispute. If you spend our time on secondary suspects, we'll both face an early retirement."

Bastide studied the *commissaire* with a quiet fury. He had never disliked anyone as he did Aynard. Perhaps, he mused for a second, his ulcers will flare up and he'll be replaced. Reality stepped in quickly to shatter the daydream. He was stuck with Aynard and he was stuck with the McCallister case.

"Be kind enough to inform me if you decide to see Député-Maire Beaulieu again," Aynard said. "I don't want further problems from him. And for God's sake, don't let Mattei near him . . . or the colonel. He can

work on the Socialists; they're more his type. Now, if you
have no questions, I must try to clear my desk."

Bastide stood up and walked to the door.

"Tell those narcotics people to come in," Aynard
called after him. "I'll have to see them before I get to
work."

Mattei was waiting when Bastide got back to his office.
"Well?" Mattei asked.

"The *commissaire* is impatient. In fact, the Ministry has
him scared. They want results and we . . . you and me
. . . are not giving them what they want."

Mattei shrugged and sat down at his desk. He ran a
small comb through his thick hair. "Is that all that's bothering him?"

"What's new?" Bastide asked.

"I've grilled JoJo's friends. Nothing. The stakeout at
the colonel's reports a series of visitors. Not very interesting. That ex-Army type Pignon spends a lot of time
with him. But there is one thing I find strange . . ."

"What's that?"

"His other visitors are surprisingly young. Well-
dressed young men in late model cars. We're checking
the licenses and hope to have some identification this
afternoon."

Bastide rubbed his chin, thinking. "He doesn't have
any children, does he?"

"No."

"These young visitors aren't butterflies are they?"

"No. I asked the same question. Macho types with
brush haircuts. Of course, that doesn't prove anything,
but from your description of the colonel I don't think
he's in the sex market . . . one way or the other."

"Interesting," Bastide commented. He picked up the Gault-Millau restaurant guide from his desk and turned the pages absently. "What else?" he asked.

"Toulon is working on the Brannec affair. In addition to Brannec's shooting skill, he seems to have been implicated in a holdup or two. He stayed at the Hôtel Rose Thé in La Ciotat just before he was found in the drink. The proprietor and the staff say he spent a great deal of time playing *boules*. They say he was a very nice man."

Bastide chuckled. "That's more than they'd say about us."

"Oh," Mattei remembered, "Janine called. She asked if you wanted to go with her to a *vernissage* at the Galerie Ouest. It's that painter you like . . . you know . . . I can't think of his name."

"Ambrogiani?"

"That's it. She wants you to call her."

"I don't have time for art galleries."

"Fine. Tell her, not me."

The report on the colonel's callers came in at five. Mattei sat at his desk, the phone secured by an upraised shoulder taking notes. Bastide made some calls. One was to the DST to ask if they had anything on Colin Napier. He never really got through to the DST, even when he had them on the line. Their task of protecting the territory of France put them in an advantageous position. If they were tired or bored or didn't want to cooperate, they simply invoked a dark secrecy full of unspoken innuendo and bureaucratic importance. There wasn't much he could do about it but it made him angry. They'd promised to run a records scan on Napier but Bastide already sensed the DST weren't eager to share whatever they might find.

Now, as Mattei continued his painstaking notes, Bastide read about a famous Parisian restaurant that Gault and Millau had crucified in their latest edition. The two epicures had been served a *pâté* that still bore the indentations of the can it had come from. Heresy! He smiled indulgently, imagining the restaurant's chef exploding in an apoplectic fit on reading their stiletto stab of criticism.

Mattei put down the telephone, his eyes on his notebook. Bastide pushed the guide aside expectantly. "What game is the colonel playing?" Mattei asked.

"Let's have it," Bastide demanded.

"Two are students. University of Aix-Marseille. Another is a junior lawyer working in Toulon. Good families . . ."

"Whatever that means."

"Well, you know . . . Papa has money." Mattei glanced at his notes. "And they have another thing in common. They're all members of Europe Uni."

Bastide stared at the ceiling, frowning slightly. "Europe Uni—isn't that a right-wing operation?"

"It is," Mattei nodded. "They've got links in Italy, Germany, Belgium, Austria and Spain. Mostly university students dedicated to saving us from ourselves and our decadent heritage of Republicanism."

"I remember. They were involved in the head cracking last year outside the Faculty of Law."

"Yes. The *cocos* crack a few heads and they crack a few heads. Unfortunately, both sides are so hard-headed that little permanent damage was done. But it's interesting . . ."

"How's that?"

"The colonel and Europe Uni. Those young hot-bloods are not known for listening to advice from their elders."

"Their visits have been regular?"

"Once a week on different days. Sometimes three of them, often only one." Mattei referred again to his notes. "Never in the house over a half hour."

Bastide nodded. "Probably want to avoid having to eat the colonel's food."

"Never more than three," Mattei continued. "Sometimes they carry briefcases. Guichard says the lawyer is a karate expert and has a hand-gun permit."

"All right. Ask Aix for detailed information on the students; run a check here. I'd like to have a report on my desk tomorrow. Names, background, the usual."

Mattei glanced at the clock and grimaced.

"I know," Bastide said, rising to stretch. "It's been a long day but if either of us leaves this office before ten tonight, I'll hear about it from Aynard. I'll get some sandwiches and beer from the canteen."

It was midnight before Bastide returned to his apartment. Once in bed he had a hard time going to sleep. A Spanish trawler moored at the *quai* was running its engine. The low rumble seemed to shake the whole apartment building. He could hear the mechanic banging on some recalcitrant valve or pipe junction. He lay with his hands behind his head and watched the shifting patterns of aqueous shadows on the ceiling. He imagined the suspects in the McCallister case as participants in a police lineup. They were definitely originals. Beaulieu, the Communist, who looked more like a *bourgeois* shopkeeper than a politician; the colonel, small and drained like the abandoned chrysalis of a multiwinged insect; the loudmouthed Senac; the testy Campi and the other Socialists, all projecting an aura of puzzled innocence. He tried to conjure up the image of Lucien Brannec and JoJo le Lièvre but they were mere wisps of imagination. It was strange how quickly the dead became transparent memories.

He shut his eyes. The suspects faded and Mireille Perraud took their place. She seemed suspended before him like a doll in a shop window and his twitching eyes moved over her nude body like fingers, savoring each soft curve and indentation. He felt himself rising, his erection pushing up the sheet. He groaned, banishing Mireille from his thoughts and rolling onto his side. As he slid off the edge of consciousness he remembered he'd forgotten to call Janine Bourdet.

It was one of those bright mornings that made the harbor of Toulon sparkle with the light and color of a Dufy watercolor. The villas and palms along the Boulevard de Faron were etched against the clear blue sky like one-dimensional stage props. A gardener was trimming a hedge and the metallic click of his clippers echoed through the empty streets.

The colonel emerged from his garden and walked purposefully along the sidewalk. His bamboo cane swung by his side. He was wearing a cheap straw hat with a wide brim that almost covered his eyes.

The plainclothes policeman in the stakeout car slid lower in his seat feigning sudden interest in a copy of *L'Express* magazine. He watched the colonel's progress with apprehension. The old man was coming directly toward him. There were only two other cars parked nearby and they were empty. The policeman propped his magazine on the steering wheel and lit a cigarette, his eyes on the colonel.

The old man drew opposite the car and paused. The policeman ignored him, looking off toward the bay. The colonel raised his cane and rapped it sharply on the car's hood.

"Good morning," he bellowed, a slight smile on his thin lips. "You can see the Porquerolles Island on a day like this."

The red-faced policeman nodded, hoping the colonel would move along. Instead he bent over and poked his head in the driver's window.

"Would you like some coffee?" he asked. "My maid could bring you a cup."

"Ah . . . no, thank you," the plainclothesman replied uncomfortably.

"Well, it must be boring for you out here. Any luck?"

"Luck?"

"Yes. You must be watching a criminal. Most unusual in this quiet neighborhood. Perhaps I can be of help?"

"Oh no, thank you."

The colonel withdrew and stood up, the flickering smile still on his face. He was enjoying himself. "If you need anything don't hesitate to call on me . . . Colonel Lebrun." He waved his cane in the general direction of his villa. "I live over there."

He turned abruptly and walked off. Several paces from the police car he chuckled aloud and swung his cane in a backhanded saber slash, beheading a sunflower that protruded above a low garden wall.

The plainclothesman watched the small retreating figure in the rear-view mirror. He waited for the colonel to disappear from sight before lifting the radio mike to send in his report.

Colin Napier sat down heavily on a flat rock and slid the small pack off his back. He wiped the perspiration from his forehead and gulped at the fresh air. It had been a hard climb. Far below, he could see his parked car and the vague square of the small cemetery. He took off his sport shirt and let the warm sun play on his pale torso. He produced binoculars from the pack and adjusted them to his eyes, panning slowly across the valley from the gorse thicket to the shrine on the far-off hill. He let the binoculars hang on his chest while he took a notebook from a pocket of his baggy khaki trousers and opened it to review his notes on what had happened that morning in 1944.

The German attack had ended at approximately nine-thirty. The Wehrmacht trucks had arrived to pick up the parachutists and their prisoners at eleven. By eleven-thirty they were gone and only the dead and a wounded McCallister remained. Whoever had taken the gold had done it between eleven-thirty in the morning and twelve midnight when Beaulieu and his FTP had found McCallister still alive. That is, if Beaulieu and his men hadn't taken the gold themselves.

Napier lit his pipe and stood up. He climbed slowly among the rocks, looking for signs of the fight. He identified an irregular string of pocks in the hard granite as probable machine-gun impacts and one overhang was marked with jagged scars that appeared to have been made by mortar fragments. He climbed atop the highest stand of granite and raised the binoculars again. There had to have been at least four men to move the gold.

That would have been the minimum because of its weight. There were probably more. He walked back to his pack, sat down and put on his shirt. The sun would turn him lobster red if he wasn't careful.

Napier had just spent two days following up on a theory one of the lads in London had dreamed up. Resistance records had shown that a wartime gang of Marseille hoods, known as "The Vultures," had made a profitable business of stealing arms, medical supplies and funds dropped to the Resistance. A faction of MI6 had considered this a plausible explanation for what might have happened at Roucas. But the theory didn't wash. The Consul General had obtained permission for Napier to review the dusty civic files on the Resistance. He'd spoken with a retired policeman who had tracked The Vultures during the war and interviewed an old British Legion member who'd had a ship chandler's shop on the Vieux Port and had known some of the gang personally. The Vultures had been decimated by a police raid three weeks before the gold was dropped and had ceased to exist as a gang.

Napier ruffled his mustache. As he saw it, the field had been narrowed to Beaulieu or the colonel. He frowned as an unwelcome thought crossed his mind. Suppose some Germans had done it? An Abwehr officer with inside information or even the Gestapo? They had been a law unto themselves. Perhaps a Gestapo agent stayed behind to investigate when the trucks left. The Gestapo would have been capable of bringing in their own transport and spiriting off the gold while the Wehrmacht was puffed with their victory and busy with prisoner interrogation. But, he remembered, that didn't wash either. Captured records had shown that the regional Gestapo had been short of agents and fully occupied in Marseille at the time.

He dug once more into his pack. The bottle of gin glinted silver in the sun. Napier smiled. "Easy," he said to himself, unscrewing the red bottle top and reaching for a plastic glass. He worked with practiced precision, mixing a gin and bitters, and leaned back on his elbows to raise his glass to the sky. "Cheers!" he said to no one in particular and took a deep swallow. Napier closed his eyes, savoring the full heat of the sun and piquant bite of the gin. He thought of all the poor bastards toiling in London and his counterparts sweating in the tropics. Well, everyone couldn't be lucky. Now all he had to do was plan a plausible approach to Colonel Lebrun. He knew it wouldn't be easy.

CHAPTER VII

It was after midnight. Most of the restaurants along the Quai de Rive Neuve were closed. The colored neon of the night clubs reflected in fluid kaleidoscope patterns on the surface of the harbor. The trawlers, three abreast, strained and groaned on their mooring lines. Bastide yawned as he walked toward his apartment building. He'd attended a retirement party for one of his detectives and he'd drunk too much wine. He had a slight headache. He was glad that Janine wouldn't be waiting for him. He paused for a moment to watch two laughing couples leave the Scotch Club and pile into their Volkswagen. They drove off weaving dangerously over the yellow median line.

"Stupid bastards," Bastide murmured, hoping a police cruiser was in the vicinity.

The receding tail lights faded from sight. The only sounds on the empty *quai* were the creaking of the hawsers, the hum of the neons and the sucking of the dark water.

Bastide crossed the street to his building. It happened unexpectedly and very fast. He was reaching for the release bell on the heavy door when he sensed a movement to his right. He swung in that direction, his hand instinctively going to his right hip for the revolver that wasn't there. There were two blasts in quick succession, split-

ting the night with red-gold fire, temporarily blinding
him. He sprawled flat on the ground and rolled away
from the door. His left forearm was numb and heavy.
Someone was running. He heard an engine start, pushed
himself up on his right elbow and watched a light-
colored sedan swing out of the Rue Font. He thought it
was a BMW but he wasn't sure. He couldn't read the
number plate. The sedan rocketed along the *quai* and
disappeared into the Rue de Chantier. Lights were coming on in the apartments above him. He rose to a kneel-
ing position and looked at his arm. The lower sleeve of
his sport coat was shredded. Warm blood was running
over his hand, dripping in viscous threads onto the pavement. He cursed and stood up unsteadily. The two impact points behind him were close together. One in the
door had gouged deep, splintered gashes in the wood.
The other had dug irregular white holes in the dark
patina of aged stone.

Then there were people. The old concierge of the
building, in her plaid robe and slippers, trying to talk
without her dentures. A fisherman from one of the trawlers who slipped off Bastide's jacket with professional
calm, ripped Bastide's shirt and applied a makeshift bandage to his arm.

"I've called the police," the owner of a nearby bar told
him. "Why don't you come in for a brandy?"

Bastide shook his head. A group of drinkers from the
Scotch Club hurried up to see the excitement, the
women whispering and giggling among themselves.

His arm started to throb. He could feel the pain walking up to his shoulder. The bar owner returned with a
glass of cognac. Bastide gulped it down. "They'll be here
soon," the bar owner said, looking off toward the Fort

Saint-Jean. "I think I hear the Klaxon now. I told them it was you."

"Thanks," Bastide murmured, realizing he hadn't really assessed the damage to his arm before the fisherman bandaged it.

The *hee-haw* of the Klaxon carried over the water and drew closer as the police ambulance sped around the Vieux Port. It arrived and executed a quick U turn, then braked directly in front of the apartment building. A gray-haired, uniformed *brigadier* jumped out of the front seat. Two attendants slid a litter out of the ambulance.

"You all right, Inspector?" the *brigadier* asked frowning.

"It's only my arm," Bastide replied.

The *brigadier* examined the blood-stained bandage. "You're losing a lot of blood. We'll get you to the hospital. Want to lie down?" he asked, indicating the litter.

"No," Bastide replied, "let's go."

A wave of dizziness hit him as he climbed into the ambulance. When the door was shut he fell back on the litter and closed his eyes.

The surgeon was a small man with very thick glasses. He worked skillfully, stitching the jagged flesh ends together. The operating table was spotted with Bastide's blood, the doctor's gown a scarlet smear. A needle taped to Bastide's right arm was supplying him with whole blood.

"Very lucky," the doctor commented, tying off a stitch. "Another inch to the right and it would have been the bone. This way it's just meat, and not too much at that. Any more would have meant a skin graft."

The door of the emergency room swung open. Mattei

appeared and paused, taking in the scene. *"Eh ba!* I knew it," he said. "Now maybe you'll listen to me."

Bastide made a vague sign of dismissal with his good arm and smiled. The anesthetic had temporarily dulled the pain. He was experiencing a light-headed feeling of relief. Mattei came forward and bent over for a better look.

"Holy mother!" He straightened up and put his hand on Bastide's shoulder. "Did you see them?"

"Only one. I'm pretty sure he was driving himself. I heard the car start after he ran away. The car looked like a white BMW."

Mattei rubbed his stubbly chin. His eyes were red and he had pulled his blazer on over his pajama top. "I'm going over to look at things. Pierre is waiting for me."

"He used both barrels," Bastide told him. "Made a mess of the door. I must have an enemy."

"More than one, Roger, more than one." Mattei reached under his jacket, withdrew a holstered Colt Cobra and put it on the table next to Bastide. "Here's your *pétard.* I'd carry it from now on if I were you, *monsieur l'inspecteur.*"

Bastide tapped the revolver with his right hand and winked at Mattei. "At your orders!"

"Good, get some rest. I'll come see you later this morning. I've put a guard on your apartment." Mattei lumbered out of the operating room as the surgeon finished his work.

"There," he said peering closely at Bastide's arm through his spectacles. "That should do it. It's going to hurt, so I'll give you some pills. Sleep will help. I've asked the nurse to give you a tetanus shot. I want to see you in twenty-four hours. Call me if you have any trouble. Still feel dizzy?"

"No."

"Well, you'll need more blood. We'll move you into a room where you can sleep and we'll keep pumping it into you."

"I'd like to go home."

"Later. Sleep first."

His eyelids were suddenly heavy. Two nurses came to escort him down the brightly lit corridor. They wheeled the transfusion rack with them, put it beside his bed and helped him undress. As he took his pills he caught a glimpse of a police uniform through the opened door. Then he slept.

It was a particular universe. He seemed to hang above it, motionless. The sky was a deep red and there was snow on the tile roofs around the Vieux Port. The water of the harbor was the color of a chocolate mousse and he could see his mother standing on the *quai* with a steaming, covered tureen in her hands. Janine and Mireille were together on his balcony like two stone statues. He had a great desire to join them but he couldn't move or cry out. As he watched, Commissaire Aynard appeared on the *quai* and called to them but they didn't respond. Aynard shrugged, turned and fell into the thick, dark water. Bastide felt himself drift lower and suddenly he was inside his apartment on the bed. He turned his head toward a murmur in the corner of the room. A faceless man was slapping Tarot cards on the floor. Janine was lying nude nearby, writhing in ecstasy, her hand between her thighs. He made a great effort to rise from the bed but he couldn't. A lassitude spread through his body. He relaxed completely letting a curtain of darkness cut him off from everyone else.

Mattei was pleased. Things had moved unaccustomedly fast. They'd found the cream-colored BMW abandoned at the Parc du Pharo. It had been stolen the evening before from the parking lot of the Aix Country Club. The owner had already reported it missing. It was being dusted for prints and searched. Mattei had slept only two hours after he'd finished at the *quai*. He hadn't found much there, not even an empty shotgun shell. Commissaire Aynard had called him in when he'd arrived at the office.

"Now, maybe you and Bastide will take this case seriously," he'd lectured. "Get on it, Mattei. I won't have my people shot at!"

The skinny, bloodless son of a bitch, Mattei had thought, he's more worried about his own ass than his people. Mattei looked at the notes he'd taken on the owner of the BMW. He was a well-to-do businessman in Aix, an accountant with his own firm. No police record, no problems. The alacrity with which he'd reported the missing vehicle indicated ignorance of any plot to use it in an assassination attempt. Mattei sat frowning at his notes. There was something tapping at the back of his mind, trying to get out. He sensed it was important but it alluded him. He put his hand to his forehead and cursed quietly. At times like this his weight and courage were of no help. But he was determined. Slowly and painfully his brain waves connected. Aix-en-Provence! Two of the colonel's visitors were from Aix. What does that prove? He stood up, put both fists into his pocket and strode around the room, thinking. He swung back to his desk, picked up the telephone and called the Police Judiciare in Aix. He asked them to check on the students to see if they or their parents were members of the Country Club. At this point any lead was worth following.

Colin Napier knew he was being followed as he turned off the Rue Paradis. His shadow wasn't very good at his trade. He was following on the same side of the street. In his eagerness not to lose Napier he was staying much too close. He was obviously an amateur. Napier turned to the right and walked toward the Opéra. He paused suddenly before a magazine rack and glanced behind him. The man almost stumbled in his attempt to slow his gait. Then, he too feigned interest in a sidewalk display of bargain shoes. Napier had taken a mental snapshot. A blue cloth cap, white shirt and work trousers, clean shaven, heavy frame, medium height, dark sideburns.

Napier continued toward the Opéra, drawing deeply on his pipe. He passed a beer truck unloading in front of a café and noted the prostitutes strung out along the street. Most of them were standing in doorways. They had young, hard faces. Some seemed to have trouble walking on their high heels. The police allowed them to operate if they didn't bother the passersby, but there was no doubt about their purpose. They displayed their wares openly with transparent blouses, slit skirts and bras that pushed their breasts up and outward like melons on a fruit stand.

He decided to have a bit of fun. The woman he selected had a ponytail of dyed blond hair, high boots of shiny red plastic, a short skirt and a black bra under a white polyester blouse. Her eyebrows were plucked and penciled above the natural growth line.

"Ah, *chéri,*" she began with a professional smile baring some badly capped teeth.

Napier stopped her. "Mademoiselle, I think we have business together."

"But, of course," she replied, winking at a colleague two doors away. "Come with me."

She led him along the sidewalk and around a corner into a narrow, shaded street. "You are not French?" she turned to ask in accented English. "American?"

"Yes. American."

She took his hand, gave it a squeeze and pulled him toward the low door of the Hôtel Delorme. She opened the door and he saw the indistinct outline of his shadower reflected on the door's window. The desk clerk, a North African in a spotted undershirt, put a key and a towel on the small reception counter. He looked at them with drug-dulled eyes, waiting.

"You pay, *chéri,* for the room."

The price was exorbitant but Napier laid out the money without protesting. It was a legitimate expense. The desk clerk snatched the franc notes before Napier could have second thoughts.

The blonde led him up a narrow staircase covered with a threadbare carpet. She opened the door, covered a yawn with a quick smile and closed the door behind them. The room smelled of disinfectant, cheap perfume and sex. There was a large pitted mirror on one wall, a stained bidet in the corner and a sagging bed. A small window looked out on the narrow street in front of the hotel.

She tried a seductive smile and took off her blouse. She came to Napier and took his pipe. "Is not good," she said teasingly. "Bad smell." She reached behind her with both hands for the clasp of her bra.

My God, Napier thought, if she releases those in this small room, I'll be forced out the bloody window! "Wait," he told her, producing his wallet once more. "I will tell you what to do," he said firmly, counting some franc notes into her outstretched palm.

"I can do anything," she said, cocking her head as if seeing him in a new light. "You want something special?"

"In a way, yes. I just want you to sit on the bed and relax. Understand?"

She shrugged. This was nothing new to her. She had experienced all kinds. She sat on the bed, watching Napier, waiting for further instructions.

He went to the window and parted the frayed curtain slightly with one finger. The man with the blue cap was there fidgeting, glancing at the hotel. Napier smiled.

"I understand," the blonde said. *"Tu te cavales.* You're on the run?"

"Not exactly," Napier replied. "Is there a back door to this hotel?"

"There is always a back door. It will take you into a yard. Go straight across the yard to the rear of the Café Tabac. Walk through the café and you are on the Rue Beauvau."

"Good. I want you to stay here for half an hour. If someone comes knocking on the door, you've never seen me."

"Wait a minute. I'm not looking for a broken face . . ."

Napier peeled a few more notes from his roll. *"Ça va?"* he asked.

"Oui," she said, pursing her lips.

"Au revoir," he said. "It's been charming," he added in English.

He was down the stairs in seconds. He found the back door behind a stack of sour-smelling wine bottles and hurried across the yard, through the rear of the café and out onto the Rue Beauvau. He turned the corner, doubling back, crossed over to the Place de l'Opéra and looked down the narrow street toward the Hôtel Delorme. Blue cap was still there puffing on a cigarette.

"Now, my friend," Napier murmured, "we'll see who has the most patience."

It was no real contest. Ten minutes later the man in the blue cap entered the hotel. He was inside six minutes before Napier saw him rush out again. Napier pulled back to keep out of sight. A heavily rouged brunette leaned toward him from her position against the wall.

"Allo, chéri!" she hissed.

"No," Napier replied shortly, "I'm quite busy."

She made an obscene gesture and turned her back.

He peered around the corner again. The blue cap was heading toward La Canebière. Napier hurried across the street and followed. It was a long walk. His quarry led him up the hill through the North African quarter, past the used clothing and luggage shops to the Place Jules-Guesde. Then he angled off toward the Gare Saint-Charles. Napier filled his pipe and lit it as he walked, keeping his eyes on the bobbing blue cap. A few more turns into narrower streets and the pace slowed. There weren't as many pedestrians about. Napier dropped back. Then he was lucky. The blue cap turned to his left and entered a three-floored, solid stone structure. Napier could see a brass plaque on the door. He waited several minutes, then walked past to read the plaque. It marked the building as the headquarters of a Communist longshoreman's union.

So, he told himself, Député-Maire Beaulieu is obviously interested in my movements. Napier hadn't expected to be put under surveillance so quickly. I suppose, he told himself, it does add a bit of spice. He paused on a busy street corner to wipe the perspiration from his brow and glanced at his watch. Close to five. Almost cocktail time.

The doctor insisted that Bastide remain in the hospital till noon the next day. A nurse brought him the morning papers with his coffee. There was a story on page three with an old file photo of Bastide. The writer must have been rushing to make the deadline for the morning edition. There wasn't much to it. "POLICE INSPECTOR WOUNDED BY UNKNOWN ASSAILANT," the head proclaimed. A paragraph of facts was supplemented by one of conjecture: "Inspector Bastide is known to have many enemies among the underworld. Was it someone he once brought to justice? Is it the result of a current investigation?" Bastide pushed the paper aside and rubbed his eyes. He shifted in the hard bed, supporting the weight of his bandaged arm with his hip. The uniformed policeman guarding his room came in to hand him a bouquet of bright wildflowers. They were from Mireille Perraud. He opened the small envelope pinned to the wax paper and read the card: "Shocked and worried. Speedy recovery. Call me. Mireille." He had just put the flowers on the bedside table when Janine arrived. He frowned, wishing someone had warned him. He didn't like being caught unprepared.

"Alors!" she said, gauging his mood. "I rush here to

see you and you receive me as if I were Commissaire Aynard." She took his head in both hands and kissed him. She looked cool and desirable in a light cotton dress and sandals.

"I'm sorry," Bastide told her. "I didn't expect you."

She sat beside him, suddenly serious. "When I heard . . . I lost a heartbeat."

He reached up to touch her neck. Then he pulled her gently to him and kissed her again. He smiled. "I'm glad to see you," he said.

"Mattei tells me it was close," she said. "They almost did it this time."

"But they didn't."

"And the arm?"

"It hurts. Some stitches. Nothing serious."

"Stop acting the brave *poulet!*" she said, suddenly angry, her eyes flashing. "You don't impress me. I'm not a naïve nursing sister."

"No," he said, chuckling, "you're not."

Then her tears came and he held her close. She straightened and blew her nose. "Who sent those?" she asked throatily.

"What?"

"The flowers."

"Oh, a friend," he said, looking for the card. Janine found it under the flowers.

"What a beautiful gesture," she said sarcastically. " 'Shocked and worried,' " she quoted. "And she wants you to call her. That's too much, the bitch. Why can't she call you. Too busy with her bridge games and Toulon society?"

"She's an old friend, Janine," Bastide said reprovingly. "You know that."

"Hah, old friend! Doesn't her stupid husband know she's dying to make love to you?" She was up now, glaring at him.

"Janine, Janine, sit down."

She paused, her hands on her hips. "I'm leaving now. They tell me you'll be out this afternoon. I'll be at your place when you get there. I'll fix a *cassoulet.*"

"Perfect. I'll be hungry by then."

She kissed him quickly on the forehead and stepped out of his reach as he tried to draw her closer.

"As to those flowers," she said, "don't bring them with you." She tried to slam the door on her way out but the automatic spring frustrated her effort.

Bastide fell back against the pillows and raised his eyes to the ceiling. "Jesus Christ in heaven!" he murmured.

Mattei was waiting for Bastide when he walked into the office. "How's your arm?"

"Sore," he replied, easing the sling and sitting down carefully.

"I think we might have something," Mattei told him.

Bastide raised his eyebrows. "Bad joke."

"It's no joke. One of those students. He's a member of the Aix Country Club."

Bastide blinked. The pain-killers made him drowsy. "So?" he asked unenthusiastically.

"The BMW was stolen there the night someone used you for target practice. The lab couldn't find any prints on the car. Signs of a quick handkerchief wipe on the wheel and the door."

"An amateur."

"Correct. A pro would have used gloves. The lab did find two cigarette butts in the ashtray. The owner doesn't smoke. Neither does his wife. This student"—Mattei glanced at a dossier on his desk—"Jean Grenier. He smokes."

"Prints, saliva?"

"They're working on it."

"Pretty thin."

"Everything we have is pretty thin. Look, this stinks of amateurism. You know, you wouldn't be sitting here if a pro had been on the trigger of that widow-maker."

Bastide nodded in agreement.

Mattei seemed to have exhausted himself. He tossed the dossier back on his desk and walked to the window. "I don't know. I just feel something about this Aix link. Europe United . . . right-wing students . . . the colonel . . . too much in one pot." He swung around. "Roger, got your *flingue?*"

Bastide flipped a corner of his jacket back to reveal a holstered revolver.

"That's better. If someone takes another shot at you, Aynard will castrate me."

"I can take care of myself. This Grenier . . . can he account for his time when I was hit?"

"I was waiting for the lab report on the butts. He comes from a good family; I didn't want . . ."

"I've heard that before." Bastide stood up and grimaced at the sudden pain. The pills weren't doing much good. "Any idea where we can find him?"

"He spends a lot of time at the Deux Garçons on the Cours Mirabeau."

"Good. Let's see if he's a conversationalist."

Mattei looked doubtful. "His parents will call Aynard in minutes if we try to push him."

"We won't be pushing him. Just a few questions.

Frankly, I'm beginning to feel something too. An old inspector who trained me referred to it as a 'whiff of shit.' We may not be directly on the scent but I think we've both had a whiff. Let's go."

The wide, tree-shaded Cours Mirabeau cuts through Aix like a royal boulevard. Ancient moss-covered stone fountains gurgle and drip in the center of the thoroughfare bisecting the slow traffic. The sun-dappled café terraces were crowded with a multiracial mix of students, tourists and local residents. Wandering musicians moved from café to café strumming guitars, imitating the nasal wailing of American folk singers and passing their hats for offerings from the seated customers. The Café les Deux Garçons is an old *aixois* tradition dating from the *belle époque.* Its wide terrace and once chic interior of aged wood, scarlet moleskin banquettes and polished brass has suffered with the passing years, but succeeding generations of students have made it their headquarters and point of rendezvous.

Mattei parked his battered Mercedes in front of the police post at the foot of the Cours Mirabeau and they walked through the heavy crowd of summer strollers to the Deux Garçons.

"Do you think he'll be here?" Mattei asked.

"We might be lucky," Bastide said, completing his examination of the drinkers at the terrace tables. "Let's go inside."

They'd both studied a picture of Jean Grenier taken by the Toulon stakeout at the colonel's. But there'd been camera movement. The print had been fuzzed and indistinct. They paused inside the door, stepping aside to let a waiter pass with a heavily loaded tray of frothing beer steins.

"There," Mattei said, nodding to a banquette in the far corner of the busy bar. A young man with short-cut blond hair was bent over a newspaper, a half-finished glass of lager in his hand.

Bastide frowned. "No," he said, "that's not him."

"I'd swear it," Mattei persisted. "Wait."

Mattei approached the reader and stood over him. "Jean Grenier?" he asked.

The young man looked up, puzzled. *"Pardon?"* he asked.

"Are you Jean Grenier?"

"No. Nils Ouverson." His accent was unmistakably Scandinavian.

"Sorry," Mattei mumbled, turning back to Bastide.

"Come on," Bastide said, "let's drop by his apartment. He might be there."

Once they were gone, a student in a Pierre Cardin suit left a noisy group of companions and walked to the public telephone near the rest room. He inserted coins, dialed a number and plugged one ear with his finger as his party answered the call.

Steam seeped from the hood of the Mercedes as they drove back to Marseille. "My God!" Bastide commented, "now what's wrong?"

"It's nothing," Mattei replied, both hands on the wheel. "It does that."

Bastide settled back in his seat and shut his eyes.

"Where do you suppose Grenier is?" Mattei asked.

"He could be shopping," Bastide said, "could be on his way to Canada."

"The landlady was helpful," Mattei remarked.

"Oh yes," Bastide said sarcastically, "Monsieur Grenier is a true gentleman. Monsieur Grenier is a very neat person. Monsieur Grenier is generous. We should have taken a look at his room."

"I don't think so. Not yet."

Bastide sat up and put on his dark glasses. "I want a wire put on the colonel's telephone," he said. "We'll have to get Aynard's approval."

"He won't like that."

Bastide shrugged. They sped along the autoroute; soon Marseille's irregular skyline came into view. They could see blue patches of the distant sea.

"What's the Englishman been up to?" Bastide asked.

"Carrying on his investigation, I guess. I haven't seen him for a few days . . ."

"Get in touch with him," Bastide said. "We should know what he's doing. He could be a hazard. Make a point of dropping by his hotel when he doesn't expect you."

"If he's soaking up gin at his usual rate, he shouldn't be too much trouble."

Someone else was interested in Colin Napier. André de Coursin of the Direction Générale de la Sécurité Extérieure had flown into Marseille earlier in the day and driven directly to the Préfecture. The DGSE had picked up unsettling rumors about the death of McCallister. Still unaware of Operation Red Gold, they had heard that Resistance funds might somehow have been involved. Napier's presence tended to confirm their suspicions.

After a brief discussion with the *préfet*, De Coursin called Commissaire Aynard to a special meeting. Aynard had had little to do with the French counterespionage

service. He resented being summoned without warning
for an unexpected meeting. He followed a shuffling
guide up the wide marble stairs of the Préfecture and
along a corridor to a small, unused office. De Coursin, a
tall gray-haired man in a well-cut dark suit, greeted
Aynard with a nod and indicated they should both sit
down. Aynard noted the rosette of a commander of the
Legion of Honor in De Coursin's lapel. He was suddenly
more receptive.

"*Mon cher commissaire,*" De Coursin began, fitting a cigarette into his onyx cigarette holder. "I thought it best
for us to meet here."

"Of course," Aynard replied, sitting on the edge of his
chair.

"I shall be brief," De Coursin continued. "For your
information alone, this Englishman Napier is not a legal
expert. He works for British Intelligence."

De Coursin lit his cigarette and extinguished the
match in an ashtray. "I would like your people to watch
him carefully. He really shouldn't be here. The British
didn't clear it with us. So, it seems he's involved in something they don't want us to know about. It could be
anything but it appears to be connected with the death of
this McCallister."

"I understand," Aynard said.

"Do you?" De Coursin raised an eyebrow. "I wish I
did. In any case, we don't want him getting into trouble.
It would be embarrassing to all concerned. Can you see
to that?"

"Yes, but . . ."

"But?"

"Your people . . . ?"

"We would rather keep our distance at the moment.

Your men are already on the case and in touch with Colin
Napier, so it makes sense to keep things on a simpler
plane."

Aynard nodded in agreement. Beneath his polite
facade he was furious. De Coursin was treating him like a
junior functionary.

"I must get back to Paris but you can pass messages to
me at any time through the *préfet,*" De Coursin continued. "I rely on you to keep this to yourself."

"Consider it done."

"Good." De Coursin stood up and extended his hand
to Aynard.

"*Au revoir,*" he said, dismissing the *commissaire.*

When Aynard had shut the door behind him, De Coursin smiled. "What an unattractive little man," he murmured, retrieving his homburg from a settee and preparing to leave.

The colonel's body was slack, sunk into the chair, but
his eyes glowed in the semidarkness of his study, darting
with quick movements from the phone to his visitor.
"You are a fool," the colonel said. "I never should have
trusted you."

Jean Grenier flinched. He was young and tan with the
air of an athlete. His jacket was of the finest camel hair.

"You acted without my authorization. How dare you!
If we were in a campaign, I'd have you shot."

"*Mon colonel,* I did it for you," Grenier murmured, not
meeting the old man's glare. It was true. He worshiped
the colonel.

"Young fools, all of you. You've risked my whole
plan," the colonel told him. "First you bungled the death
of the sharpshooter. Then this attack on Bastide! The

theft of the car was particularly stupid." He tapped the desk with his thin hand. "They were looking for you in Aix. Do you realize what that means? No, you probably don't. You are no longer of use to me. You shouldn't have come here."

"I believe in our cause," Grenier said, lifting his head. "I would die for it."

"Ha! How dramatic. At this rate you probably will." The colonel shifted his position with the careful precision of an arthritic. He reached into a drawer and put an envelope on the desk. "You are to take this money," he said. "Leave immediately for Austria. Contact Gerhardt in Vienna. He will take care of you. You may have to go on to Italy. Don't even think of coming back to France till you hear from me."

"What will you do?"

"What will I do? First I will think and then I will act. Thanks to you I no longer have the luxury of time. There is a policeman in a car outside. I'm sure he's reporting your visit. Now, Grenier, you must go."

Grenier took the money and stood up. "Sir, I . . ."

"Out!" the colonel bellowed, pointing toward the door.

He was disappointed in Grenier. He'd badly misjudged the young man's character. He'd selected Grenier among all the others to step in if anything happened to him. Sealed instructions addressed to Grenier were in the colonel's safe-deposit box at the Banque de France. They contained precise instructions for Grenier, to follow in the event of the colonel's death. Only one other member of the group, the lawyer from Aix, knew of the instructions, that they were to be delivered to Grenier. Now Grenier was out of it.

The colonel savored the silence in the dark room. His thin hand lifted a Lucite paperweight with a jagged piece of shrapnel in its center. The doctors had dug it out of his thigh in Germany after the fighting for Durlach.

He put the paperweight down and sighed, remembering that night and morning at Roucas in 1944. He'd led a patrol of three men to observe the activities of the Réseau Renard. The colonel had considered it essential to watch the other Resistance groups. A simple matter of security.

From their hiding place he and his men had watched the whole drama with night glasses: the air drop; the strange moves of McCallister and the sergeant as they worked till first light burying something near the shrine and camouflaging the site of another cache. When the Englishman returned to the ridge the colonel had been ready to descend into the valley for a closer look but then the German attack had begun.

It had been a strange experience to watch the action, like a tactical exercise at the infantry school. But the rattle of firing, the explosions, the death and the wounds had been real.

The colonel frowned, recalling the German victory. The defenders, under the command of the Englishman, had been slow to react. When they had, it had been a sloppy performance. As much as he disliked Socialists, it had pained him to see Frenchmen die uselessly. His anger had grown as the German parachutists moved closer to the stony hill crest. He had almost ordered his men to fire but his professionalism would not allow it. He would not sacrifice his men because others had been stupid.

Then he had seen the Englishman running from the fight. It had been too much for the colonel. Overcome by a searing hate, he'd ordered his men to cover him. He remembered sliding down the slope, dry stones rolling and bouncing ahead. The firing on the crest had slackened as he'd reached the flat ground to find McCallister hiding in the gorse. What a coward that man had been!

The colonel closed his eyes, reliving the moment. He'd raised his Mauser Parabellum as the Englishman turned toward him. The colonel's single shot, lost in a burst of fire from the hill, had thrown the Englishman into the bushes. He'd stepped forward to put a bullet in McCallister's skull. A sudden silence had stopped him. The fighting had ended. German parachutists were calling to each other. There was the sound of movement. He'd stooped to retrieve McCallister's revolver and had seen the gold. He'd kicked at the soft earth and found more. Then there were Germans nearby. He'd left the gorse patch hurriedly, scrambling back up the slope, using a small oak-shielded ravine as cover.

The colonel opened his eyes and cleared his throat. He'd made two major errors that day. Pride in his marksmanship had blinded him to the fact that McCallister was still alive. He had not returned to the gorse to confirm McCallister's death. When the Germans had left with their prisoners he'd sent two men to explore the find of coins while he'd climbed to the shrine with a third man to dig for the buried canister.

Racing against time they'd dragged the heavy canister into the next valley and concealed it under the roots of a dead tree. Gathering the other gold was more difficult. His men had worked steadily, filling the smashed canister with rolls of coins, manhandling it up the slope and down to the dead tree that stood like a gray finger above the greener foliage. They'd made three trips while he'd remained at the tree, digging a hole to hide their find. His men had asked if he wanted McCallister buried. The colonel had refused. "He doesn't deserve burial," he'd told them.

He'd predicted the Englishman's return would cause trouble. There was no doubt in his mind that McCallister had been sent by British Intelligence to find who had the gold. They'd tried before and failed. After all those years they'd failed again. McCallister was finally dead. The colonel had one regret. The three men who had helped him with the gold, who had kept his secret, were no longer with him. Bertaud had not come back from Indochina in 1954, Cagne had died of a heart attack eight years later and Godoy was in the Foreign Legion veterans' home, more a vegetable than a man. But that was all ancient history.

There was so much to do, so little time left. He forced himself to be lucid and objective. It was too late to brood about errors. Now it was a question of speed and efficiency. If they were already looking for Grenier, they'd soon be coming for him. He knew he was expendable but the cause was not. So many years of work for a new Europe. A Europe of strength and pride built on strong, authoritative governments and a disciplined populace. He had not been alone. His influential contacts spread from Scandinavia to Italy, from England to Germany. All of them shared the same dream, working toward the day when the weak, parliamentary regimes of compromise would be swept aside and replaced in each nation by a new generation of dedicated, hard leaders. Now he had made mistakes. Perhaps it was age. He should never have allowed his young acolytes so much freedom. But looking back never helped. He cleared his throat and sat up straight in his chair. He would make his contribution now.

He reached for his cane and rose from the desk. He could hear his housekeeper working in the kitchen. He moved quietly out of his study and down the hall, flicked on the light to the basement and descended the stairs carefully. It was a musty, cluttered cave heavy with years of accumulated dust, empty packing cases and the frame of an old bicycle. The light from a bare bulb by the door projected the colonel's gnomelike shadow over the stone floor. He locked the door carefully behind him, throwing a huge bolt in place, walked to a corner of the room, put his cane down and pushed two of the packing cases to one side. Panting, he fell to his knees and scraped at the dusty stones until he found one with an iron ring imbedded in its surface. He tugged at the ring till the stone moved. He pulled it toward him, puffing and gasping for breath. The stone rose slowly till he could rest it on the floor. His hands were shaking but he gathered his strength once more and pushed it to one side. He leaned forward on his elbows and peered into the small, dark hole. At first he saw nothing. Then, as his tired eyes became accustomed to the shadows he could make out the forms of the small, filled sacks.

Thirty-eight long years! He had been tempted to use the gold before. When Indochina fell in 1954 he'd hoped for a right-wing backlash against the government of Mendès-France. It hadn't come. He'd almost used the gold after the revolt of the generals in Algiers in 1961, but his contact with the clandestine Organisation de l'Armée Secrète had left a bad taste in his mouth. He'd considered them thugs and amateurs.

He would have preferred waiting a bit longer to give

the Mitterand government more time to prove its incompetence and to improve his own organization, but now he had no choice. Ironically, the relentless and unforgiving British had forced his hand. At least, he told himself, I am still alive and able to participate.

He spoke to the inanimate gold as if it were an old acquaintance. "Finally," he sighed, "you are going to play the role meant for you."

CHAPTER VIII

The stakeout had reported Grenier's departure from the colonel's villa. Bastide and Mattei no sooner arrived in Marseille than they found themselves on the road back to Aix. This time they traveled fast in an unmarked police sedan swerving from lane to lane on the autoroute and using their Klaxon at intersections.

The door to Grenier's apartment was unlocked. "Planning a trip?" Bastide asked him. Mattei was ready in a backup position in the hall.

"Who are you?"

"Bastide, Police Judiciare." He walked into the room noting the hurried preparations for departure. He saw an envelope, a passport and a small notebook on the dresser. He picked them up.

"One minute," Grenier shouted, "you have no . . ."

"Shut up," Mattei ordered, coming into the apartment.

Bastide flicked the pages of the passport, paused at Grenier's photo and glanced up at him. He riffled through the franc notes in the envelope. "Enough for a very good time." He dropped the envelope and passport on the dresser and began to examine the notebook.

"Sit down," Mattei told Grenier, indicating the bed. "You make me nervous."

Bastide found the notebook filled with names and telephone numbers in Austria, Italy, Sweden, Germany, Spain and Belgium.

There was something Mattei did not like in Grenier's manner. He moved closer to watch him more carefully. "Look out!" Mattei shouted, lunging toward Grenier.

Grenier was struggling to disentangle a shotgun he'd pulled from under the bed. Mattei's bulk crushed him into the mattress. Bastide's Colt was leveled at Grenier's forehead. Grenier released the shotgun. It fell on the floor.

"You miserable bastard," Mattei growled, twisting Grenier's arm behind him. "I'll bite your ear off."

Bastide holstered his weapon, picked up the shotgun and removed the shells. He turned it in his hands and shook his head. "We meet again."

Mattei looked over his shoulder at Bastide. "Same gun?"

"Could be. I just felt a significant twinge in my left arm. Let's take him in."

"He's very handsome," Mattei commented. "Probably look more mature without all his teeth."

"Take it easy," Bastide cautioned. "As you say, he comes from a good family."

They were back in Marseille by 5 P.M. The questioning began immediately. They used the Ping-Pong method. Bastide and Mattei sat at opposite ends of the small cell throwing questions in turn. An experienced criminal would have kept his eyes on the floor or focused at a spot on the wall, but Grenier swiveled his head from one to the other, trying to keep up with their rapid-fire queries.

Jean Grenier's past hadn't prepared him for the realities of police procedure. The good schools, the country club, the weekends at a family *château* were of no use now.

Mattei's sudden detailing of the charges he was likely to face hit Grenier hard. He drew in on himself like a snail under salt. Bastide and Mattei exchanged a significant glance.

"The only one who can help you now is yourself," Bastide told him. "To us, it's simple. You're an assassin with at least one successful hit and two misses . . . both attempts on the lives of police officers."

"My lawyer . . ." Grenier began, his voice shrill.

"Forget your lawyer. You're dealing with us. You just tried to kill us, remember?"

"I didn't. I wouldn't have fired . . ."

Mattei laughed briefly. "Like you did from the ridge?"

"I didn't," Grenier pleaded, rubbing his thumbs nervously along his forefingers. "I didn't kill the Englishman!"

Bastide got up and approached Grenier. "You make me sick," Bastide said quietly. "Look at you. Well dressed, well fed, a home, money, a future and here you are. Inspector Mattei and I see a lot. We deal with criminals who've been on the street since they were twelve. At least they have some excuse. Their families are a mess. Their old men dumped them, their mothers are hustlers, they scrounge for the next meal and end up in a garbage bin with a knife between their ribs in some stupid argument over a handful of francs. We don't like these people. We understand them. You, you're a different case."

"Why did you kill McCallister?" Mattei asked, jolting Grenier upright in his chair.

"I didn't. It . . . wasn't me."

"I suggest it's time for you to talk seriously," Bastide said, sitting down again. "Tell us about the colonel."

Grenier cleared his throat. Perspiration shone on his forehead. "Can I go to the toilet?"

"Later," Bastide replied.

"The colonel," Grenier began in a whisper, "he . . ."

"Speak up!" Mattei demanded.

"The colonel is like the soul of France," Grenier said, stiffly.

Bastide raised his eyebrows. "Go on," Mattei told Grenier.

"He wanted to protect this country from the Communists . . . and the fools . . ."

"Shit!" Mattei interrupted. "Just answer my questions and forget the propaganda. Who killed McCallister?"

"A sharpshooter."

"Which sharpshooter?"

"Lucien Brannec."

"And you killed Brannec."

"Not me."

"Who did?"

"I'm not sure."

"I don't believe you. Why was he killed?"

"The colonel . . ."

"Yes, go ahead."

"The colonel said it was necessary. All links to McCallister's death had to be . . . erased." Grenier paused for a second or two. "It was for the good of the cause," he continued. "McCallister's return could have ruined everything."

"What is 'everything'?"

"Our movement. Our role in the new Europe. The rebirth of France."

"There he goes again," Mattei commented.

"An old madman and a few spoiled students were

going to change the face of France?" Bastide shook his head. "You expect us to believe that?"

Grenier rose to Bastide's taunting. There was the slight hint of defiance in his voice. "We weren't alone. We have friends. The colonel has . . . resources."

"What resources? Arms? Money? Foreign backing?"

"I don't know."

"You worked with him and you didn't know?"

"It was his secret. He said we'd know when the time came. The colonel has enough resources to command respect."

Mattei opened his notebook and read from a page. "Respect from Europe Nouveau? From the Black International? From the fascist brotherhood?"

Grenier was silent. Bastide walked to the door. "Come on, Mattei. We'll let him think for a while."

"I've got to go to the toilet," Grenier pleaded.

"All in good time, *mon petit,*" Mattei replied, slamming and locking the cell door. "Watch this pigeon," he told a uniformed policeman in the corridor. "He may try something stupid."

"Come on," Bastide said, hurrying toward his office. "I smell more that a whiff now. We've got to move fast."

"How about the wire on the colonel's villa?"

"Too late."

"Are you going to tell Commissaire Aynard about Grenier?"

"Look, if Grenier was just at the colonel's, the old son of a bitch probably knows our stakeout spotted him. He could also know we've been after Grenier. That's probably why Grenier was leaving. We could lose the colonel if we don't hurry. Forget Aynard. Tell Pierre to follow us with another inspector and get on the radio to Toulon.

I'll tell them exactly what we need once we're on the road."

Mattei turned and rushed off down the corridor while Bastide pushed open his office door. There was one message lying in the center of his desk. A brief transcript of the last report from the stakeout. It had been received a half hour earlier. A stranger had arrived at the colonel's villa. The stakeout reported he couldn't identify the caller but he was smoking a pipe, had a ruddy complexion, extremely bushy, white eyebrows and could "be an Englishman."

Bastide cursed quietly. He had sensed Napier would be a problem from the beginning. He stuffed the message into his jacket pocket, left his office and hurried down the grimy staircase.

Colin Napier was nursing a bruised ego. Walking across the threshold of Colonel Lebrun's villa to find himself nose to muzzle with a cocked automatic in the hands of the old man was bad enough. To have been pushed to the floor and tied securely by a gray-haired housekeeper was humiliating.

He shifted his cramped position in a corner of the colonel's cellar and tried to take a deep breath. The tapes over his eyes and his mouth were tight. The cords securing his feet and hands well knotted. The whole process had taken only a few minutes. The colonel had not addressed one word to him. He'd obviously called at the wrong time. The old boy had the wind up for some reason. Things would undoubtedly get worse.

Upstairs the colonel completed his call to Aix and put down the telephone. He'd used prearranged code words to speak to his young supporters, asking for immediate help and requesting two light, covered trucks. He put his thin veined hands to his forehead massaging his temples, thinking. It wasn't easy being in action again. His thoughts didn't move that fast. His weak bowels were growling.

"The policeman," he murmured aloud, "that's it." The stakeout must be removed.

He called his housekeeper and explained her next duty. She listened, a stolid, unimaginative Alsatian, extremely loyal to her employer.

"You understand?" the colonel asked when he'd finished. She nodded and shuffled out the front door.

The detective in the stakeout car was reading a racing form. He looked up, surprised to see the housekeeper hurrying toward him waving a soiled dishcloth. He opened the car door as she reached him.

"What is it?" he asked.

"The colonel. He's had an attack. He needs help."

He flicked off the switch of the static-filled police radio and vaulted out of the sedan to follow the housekeeper.

"Hurry," she urged.

The colonel was waiting in the hall shadows. "Don't move," he rasped, his automatic pressed to the base of the detective's skull. The detective froze.

"This is not possible," he said, incredulous.

"It is, young man. Marie, take his gun. That's it, give it to me. Now, down on the floor, flat, hands and legs extended. *Voilà*, that's it."

"You mustn't do this," the detective remonstrated. "I . . ."

"Silence! You are more or less innocent in this matter. I don't want to hurt you." He motioned the housekeeper forward. "Tape his mouth and eyes. We'll tie him up in the cellar."

The two police cars careened from the courtyard of the Hôtel de Police, Klaxons blaring, skidded over the cobblestones and headed through the thick evening traffic toward the entrance of the autoroute to Toulon. Mattei was driving the lead sedan, cursing, swinging the wheel and braking like a driver at the Monte Carlo Rallye. Bastide was testing the radio, making contact with control and asking them to raise the Police Judiciare in Toulon. The two detectives in the second car were having trouble keeping up with Mattei. A white Kharman Ghia driven by an attractive blonde ignored the Klaxoning and pulled in front of Mattei.

"*Conasse!*" he bellowed, hitting the brakes and trying to control a skid. He spun the wheel and swung free, narrowly missing a pedestrian on the edge of the sidewalk. Once on the wide Avenue du Prado things were better. Most of the drivers were heeding the Klaxon and pulling over.

"We should have called for the helicopter," Mattei said, wiping the perspiration from his eyes.

"We'd have needed Aynard's clearance for that," Bastide replied. "Two hours of explanation and argument. *Bon sang!*" he cursed, tapping the radio. "Where is Toulon?"

"We won't hear them till we're closer. Too much distance, too many mountains."

"You say the Englishman was there," Mattei asked, "at the colonel's?"

"That was the report."

"Bad timing."

"Very bad. Monsieur Napier may be in trouble. He should have stayed in London, bowler and all."

The radio came alive once they'd passed Les Lecques. The orange sun was sinking into the Mediterranean and one thin fluffy cloud hung like golden wool over the mountains. Marseille control patched Bastide into the PJ office in Toulon. Sous-Inspecteur Guichard came on, relaxed and insouciant as ever.

"*Salut,* Bastide! Understand it's urgent."

"It is. This is a big one. It's the colonel. Up to his ass in the McCallister case. There's also an Englishman in danger."

"*Oh là, là!*" Guichard said, clucking his tongue.

"Exactly. Listen, we're short of time. I want the street approaches to the colonel's villa sealed. No one in or out."

"Understood. You'll need my men?"

"Not too many. Have them close the streets and keep out of sight. I'll talk to them when I arrive."

"I'll meet you there."

"Very well. Bring some tear gas and a marksman. Tell your men to be on the lookout for any friends of the colonel's, particularly young men in sports cars."

"Done. Is that all?"

"For the moment. Put someone on this radio. We don't want to lose contact."

"Till later . . ."

"*Au revoir.*"

Bastide put the mouthpiece on his lap and unfolded a map of Toulon. He wanted to find the street that would put them as close to the colonel's villa as possible without being seen.

Bastide had already lost his race with some of the colonel's men. A red Ferrari was parked in front of the villa, its overheated engine clicking after the fast trip from Aix. The colonel was seated behind his desk dressed for travel in an old khaki hunting coat and baggy cotton trousers. His two visitors were standing, waiting for the colonel to complete his examination of the desk's drawers. They wore blue jeans, tennis shoes and light jackets. They kept glancing out the window and exchanging looks of exasperation.

The colonel banged his desk drawer shut and sighed. He surveyed the study, his eyes lingering on his collection. His whole life was there: Saint Cyr . . . 1940 . . . Africa . . . the Resistance. He sighed again and got up, clearing his throat.

"Well, Georges," he asked, "where are the trucks?"

"They'll be here soon," the tall youth with dark hair replied. "They left Aix immediately after your call."

"As planned?" the colonel demanded.

"Yes, *mon colonel.*"

"And the plane?"

"Nicolas has been alerted. He will have the bimotor ready at the Hyères-Plage private field. He's filed a flight plan to Monaco. The papers are in order for Italy. General Bernadetto has been alerted. He'll be waiting at Alassio with some of his people. There should be no problems with customs."

The colonel smiled. Italy was the best choice. Belgium was too far away, Germany security was too tight and the movement in Spain was too disorganized. The government in Italy was about to fall again, the security forces were fully occupied with terrorism and the retired General Bernadetto had the best right-wing organization in

Europe. His network could insure quick and efficient use of the gold.

"We must be careful at Hyères," the colonel cautioned. "We will be vulnerable while loading."

"The bimotor is in a hangar, out of public view," Georges explained. "We can do it quickly."

"Are you armed?" the colonel asked.

Gilbert, a nineteen-year-old with a fuzzy blond mustache, raised his jacket to reveal the butt of a Bernardelli automatic protruding from his belt. Georges produced a Llama .32 from his jacket pocket.

"Good," the colonel told them, patting the Beretta in the deep pocket of his hunting coat. "Now, come with me. We must start moving our cargo. It will be hard work." He led them down to the cellar, unlocked the door and switched on the light. The visitors saw the two prisoners stretched out on the stone floor. Their eyes widened.

"Snoopers," the colonel explained. "One of them British. Probably a hired killer. Their intelligence service stops at nothing. But don't let them distract you. Come."

"Are . . . are they injured?" Georges asked.

"No, no. Not even a bruise. Hurry now, over here." The colonel directed them to lift the loose stone by its ring. "One sack at a time," he told them. "They're very heavy."

Gilbert lifted the first sack with both hands, straining to bring it out of the cache. *"Mon dieu!"* he exclaimed. "It's like lead. What is it?"

"Our insurance," the colonel smiled. "Take them upstairs and pile them in the hall. We don't want to waste time when the trucks get here."

Georges stared at the men on the floor. Napier shifted his position and Georges started involuntarily.

"Hurry up," the colonel admonished. "Get to work." The two youths struggled up the stairs with their loads. The colonel rubbed his hands together slowly. All his planning and the long years of waiting would soon be ended. He would be ready to take his place as a recognized leader in the movement. His contacts in Brussels, Vienna and the other capitals would take him seriously now. The gold insured it. He turned to Napier and the detective. They didn't realize it, he thought, but they were participating in a historic event. "A new Europe," he murmured to himself. "A Europe purged of scum."

The jangling phone tore Député-Maire Jean Beaulieu away from paperwork. He put down his pen, rubbed his eyes and picked up the receiver.

"Monsieur?" his caller said. "It's Jean."

"Ah, Jean, what's new?"

The man in the blue cloth cap detailed Napier's movements up to the moment he had entered the colonel's villa.

"It's very strange," he continued. "He's been in there a long time. After that, an old woman came out and called in a *flic* who was sitting outside in his car. Then two young men arrived in a Ferrari. No one has come out since."

Beaulieu pursed his lips. "It seems something is happening," he said, reflectively. "Where are you now?"

"I'm phoning from a café. I don't like the look of things."

Beaulieu nodded. "I agree. We should not become involved. Don't return to the villa. Go back to Marseille."

"And tomorrow?"

"I think it is out of our hands. I will call if you're needed."

"As you wish. Good night."

"Good night, Jean." Député-Maire Beaulieu put the telephone down slowly. He would like to know what was happening. It would be too great a risk to have Jean return to the villa. Perhaps, he mused, picking up his pen, we are reaching the denouement of *l'affaire* McCallister. He couldn't concentrate on his work. The specter of his role in Operation Red Gold was still there to haunt him.

Mattei cut the Klaxon as they turned onto the Boulevard du Faron. "Turn left," Bastide directed him, the map in his hand. "Now right." The other police car was close behind them. "Slow down," Bastide said. "Now," he shouted, "Pull in behind those cars."

Guichard was there in the beam of their lights, waving them down. One of his cars was blocking the street. Two small trucks had been stopped. Guichard's men had the occupants braced over the hoods, their legs apart.

"Just in time," Guichard said, smiling. "Look what we've found. Six young adventurers."

Bastide and Mattei exchanged handshakes with Guichard and walked with him to the prisoners. "They were armed, one with an Armalite. Bad boys, I'd say."

"Any identification?" Bastide asked.

"Yes. All from Aix. Four have student cards from the university."

Mattei took a close look at each of them. "No familiar faces. All clean cut and military, in the colonel's image," he said. "My God, this one is wearing camouflage parachutist's gear."

Bastide was silent, looking at the trucks. The colonel was planning to move or to move something. "Can you clear them out of here?" he asked Guichard.

"I'll have them taken in."

"Good. Do you have the gas and the marksman?"

"Right here," Guichard said, indicating a team of four policemen standing by the blocking sedan. Bastide could see the dull sheen of the stumpy gas gun and the long barrel of the sniper's rifle.

"Everything's blocked," Guichard told him. "They can't get away in a vehicle. The house is being watched, front and rear. I think they've got my stakeout in there. Be careful."

Bastide fingered his mustache, watching the prisoners being led to a police van. "Come on," he said. "It's time to visit the colonel."

All the gold was stacked in the hall. Georges and Gilbert were resting. The colonel was pacing slowly back and forth.

"They're late," he remarked accusingly. "Not dependable at all."

He'd been reviewing his next moves carefully. It would be a pleasure to watch General Bernadetto's reaction when he revealed what he could suddenly contribute to the cause. He knew they'd tolerated him for his age and experience but they had never taken him too seriously. He had been useful in minor ways—organizing right-wing students and assisting the movement's agents when they passed through France. It would be different now. The gold wasn't a fortune but it would be very useful. It could buy arms and people and finance operations. Only through him would they obtain it. And it was British gold . . . meant for the Socialists. He chuckled. Retribution and justice!

The colonel's neighbor was alarmed and uneasy. He let Bastide and his men in after they'd flashed their credentials. Luckily, he'd been alone reading his evening paper when they'd banged on his back door. The kitchen smelled of grilled meat and there were unwashed dishes piled in the sink. The house was across the street from the colonel's villa. The front windows offered a good view.

"You have a telephone?" Bastide asked.

"Yes," the neighbor said in a whisper, as if he were already part of a conspiracy. "There, by the couch."

Bastide found the colonel's number in his notebook and dialed it. The phone rang six times before anyone answered.

"*Allo?*" It was the housekeeper.

"I wish to speak with Colonel Lebrun," Bastide said forcefully.

"He is not here."

"This is Inspector Bastide. I *know* the colonel is there. Tell him to come to the phone immediately."

Mattei came into the room. "I've placed the marksman and the gas gun," he told Bastide. Bastide nodded, the phone pressed to his ear. He removed it and put his hand over the mouthpiece.

"You told them not to fire without our orders?"

"Certainly."

"*Allo!* Bastide? What is this? I am very busy." The colonel's voice was gruff and unfriendly.

"Listen to me carefully, Colonel Lebrun. Everything is finished."

"Finished? You must be mad. What game is this? I'll report you to your superiors."

Bastide cleared his throat. "I want you and everyone in the villa to come out, hands above your heads and unarmed. Do you understand?"

"This is impossible! Do you realize who you're talking to?"

"*Mon colonel*, you have ten minutes."

"Where are you?"

"You have exactly ten minutes beginning . . . now."

Bastide could hear the old man's breathing for a few seconds before the line was cut off.

The colonel turned toward Georges, his face purple. "Who was it?" Georges asked.

"The enemy, you fool!" the colonel bellowed. "Oh, if only I had some good men." He picked up his cane and tapped it on his shoe. "I must think," he said aloud. "We must make the best of this."

Gilbert stood close behind Georges. "What's wrong?" he whispered. Georges gestured for him to be silent.

To them the colonel seemed transfixed, staring at the waist-high pile of bags. He suddenly braced his hunched shoulders and turned to them. "We must set an example," he said with renewed vigor. "It is our only choice. We must resist."

Georges swallowed hard and glanced at the front door. "*Mon colonel*, is it the police?"

"Yes." The colonel walked into his study. He opened his desk drawer and pocketed the automatic he'd taken from the detective.

"Marie!" he called to the housekeeper. "Go down to the cellar and stay there."

When he returned to the hall his eyes were shining, his thin face still flushed. "Gentlemen, consider yourselves fortunate," he told them. "We shall make history tonight."

Gilbert shifted uneasily.

"They undoubtedly have us surrounded," the colonel continued. "No use trying a sortie. We'll fight it out here."

"But he's crazy!" Gilbert whispered to Georges.

The phone rang. The colonel walked to it and ripped the cord from the wall. "Turn out all the lights," he ordered. "Quickly now . . . Georges, you are responsible for the front approaches. Gilbert, you take the rear. I shall move between you depending on the need." He drew his Beretta, chambered a round and indicated they do the same. They obeyed with a marked lack of enthusiasm.

Bastide and Mattei could see the lights go out from their position across the street. They had left the house and were crouched behind a thick hedge. Guichard had ordered the street lights cut off. The neighborhood was silent under the faint glow of a rising moon. A policeman wearing a bullet-proof vest edged his way over to them and handed Bastide a portable loud-hailer. Mattei motioned the man with the gas gun forward and indicated the largest window in the front of the house. The marksman was already in place on the second floor of the house they'd just left.

"The damn fool isn't coming out," Mattei whispered.

Bastide nodded. He raised the loud-hailer, snapped a

switch and lifted it to his mouth. "Colonel Lebrun," he said, "your time is . . ." He stopped. There was no amplification, only a dull buzzing from the loud-hailer.

"*Putain!*" Mattei cursed. "The battery is dead."

Bastide put the loud-hailer aside. He cupped his hands and shouted toward the villa.

"Colonel Lebrun! Your time is up. Come out now. Hands above your heads!"

The pistol shots popped like firecrackers. Bastide, Mattei and the other policemen hugged the ground.

"*Les salauds!*" Mattei cocked his Colt. "Let me go in after them."

"Easy, Babar," Bastide cautioned. "I want no one hurt."

He turned to the man with the gas gun. "*Allez!* Put one through the window."

The gunner rose to one knee, aimed carefully and fired. The gun thunked hollowly. The crash of shattering glass echoed along the deserted street. Three defiant shots from the villa snapped over their heads. Guichard crawled up to them with two gas masks. "You'll need these if you're going in there," he said. "We'll see," Bastide replied, keeping his eyes on the closed door.

Georges had followed the colonel's instructions and soaked some face towels in the bathroom sink. They wrapped them around their heads, covering their mouth and nose, retreating from the front room.

"Stay close to the floor," the colonel gasped. He rose on his knees and fired out the shattered window, holding the automatic above his head.

The gas canister was still hissing by the couch, sending out an acrid plume of blue-gray smoke. The colonel tapped Gilbert on the shoulder. "Pick it up with your towel and throw it out the window."

Gilbert remained motionless. Georges threw a towel over it and tossed it out the window. As he turned back to the hall there was a thump outside. A second hot canister tumbled into the living room and hit Georges in the small of the back, knocking him flat.

He was semiconscious for a few seconds, long enough for the canister to set his trousers smoldering. The colonel crawled to him and kicked the canister away. The gas was heavy now and the damp towels were of little use. Their eyes were like burning coals. They were all retching, their stomach muscles tightened with involuntary seizures. Instinctively, like wounded giant tortoises, they crawled slowly toward the rear of the house, away from the gas. Before he left the hall the colonel turned and blindly emptied the clip of his automatic at the front door.

Bastide couldn't risk his men further. "Babar," he told Mattei, "Have the marksman put a few rounds through the door. Then we'll go in."

Mattei left, running in a crouch. Bastide turned to the policeman with the gas gun. "Let them have another." He pulled on the gas mask, leaving it on his forehead, free of his face, and drew his revolver.

The marksman fired from the second floor, the report of the high-powered rifle like a whiplash. Chips and splinters flew from the front door as he sent five rounds into the villa. Two detectives were already across the street, concealed in the garden. Mattei came back, puffing, and crouched expectantly beside Bastide. He pulled on his gas mask. "Let's go," Bastide murmured.

They were across the street in seconds, covered by the marksman and the other policemen. They paused on each side of the door, revolvers held shoulder high, their fingers on the triggers. Mattei stepped forward and kicked the door off its hinges. He held his Colt with both hands covering Bastide as he moved carefully into the hallway. The gas, a gray swirl, clung to the eyepieces of the masks, making it difficult to see more than five feet ahead. At first Bastide thought the hall had a yellow carpet. Then his feet hit the metal. The marksman's shots had ripped into two of the sacks. The coins had cascaded onto the floor in a golden torrent. As Bastide moved toward the rear of the house he heard Mattei's muffled curse of astonishment.

The colonel, Georges and Gilbert were prostrate in the kitchen. Bastide opened the back door. A gas-masked detective was waiting outside. Mattei began opening windows to clear the gas. He searched the prisoners for weapons but found none. They'd dropped their automatics as they'd crawled along the hall. Mattei sent the detective to retrieve them. Guichard and two of his men arrived. They went to work opening all the other windows in the villa. The draft drove the gas out like smoke from a cooking fire. Mattei lifted his mask cautiously and blinked his eyes.

"It's all right now," he told them.

Guichard stopped short in front of the gold. "Holy mother!" he said. "Ali Baba's cave!"

Bastide had the colonel by the collar. "Where's the Englishman?" he demanded. He pulled the colonel into a sitting position. The old man was retching, fighting for breath. Bastide lifted him and dragged him into the back yard. Mattei found the door to the cellar. Two policemen helped him smash it in.

"Roger!" he called. "Come."

Bastide left the colonel slumped against a tree. "Watch him," he told Guichard. He joined Mattei to rush down the stairs.

"Here's your Englishman," Mattei said, crouching down to remove the tape from Napier's eyes and mouth. Bastide did the same for the detective. Another policeman led the housekeeper outside.

"Ouch," Napier protested. Some of his eyebrows and the hairs of his mustache had come off with the tape. "By God," he said, "I'm glad to see you." They untied the prisoners and helped them to their feet.

"Let's go upstairs," Bastide suggested.

Guichard appeared at the doorway. "Bastide, *mon vieux!*" he hissed in warning. "Commissaire Aynard's here."

"Oh, *merde!*" Mattei growled, helping Napier up the stairs.

Commissaire Aynard was in the living room, holding a handkerchief over his mouth and nose.

"Bastide!" he called. "I want to talk with you."

He led the way out the front door to the garden. Bastide followed, his face set. He wasn't sure what was coming. He was determined not to take any more from Aynard even if it meant a transfer or a demotion. Aynard stopped under one of the palms and folded his handkerchief.

"Why was I not told of this operation?" the *commissaire* asked.

"We had no time."

"Something as important as this?" Aynard gestured

toward the house and the busy detectives. "You think because it's been a success I won't reprimand you? You don't know me."

"*Monsieur le commissaire,* I *do* know you."

"I warn you, Bastide . . ."

"Aynard!" A tall, gray-haired man in a dark double-breasted suit had come up the walk. Two younger men were with him.

"Oh," Aynard said deferentially, "Monsieur de Coursin."

The gray-haired man came closer. Bastide had heard of André de Coursin, a legendary figure in the French intelligence service.

"*Monsieur le commissaire,*" De Coursin explained, "I'm afraid I must break up this little party quickly. I've come to take the colonel and the gold. I'll leave the other prisoners with you."

Aynard was furious. "Impossible!" he replied, his voice cracking. "This is a police matter. My men have broken the case. You have no right . . ."

De Coursin frowned at Aynard. "Jacques," he called to one of his men. "The documents, please."

He took the small dossier, unfolded some papers and handed them to Aynard. De Coursin's assistant held a small flashlight so Aynard could read them.

"*Mon cher* Aynard," De Coursin explained, "we don't have time to argue. The press will be here any moment. It is a very delicate affair. We must keep problems to a minimum."

Bastide caught a glimpse of the papers over Aynard's shoulder. One was on the letterhead of the Élysées Palace. The other bore the signature of the Minister of the Interior.

Aynard's attitude underwent an abrupt change. His manner was now obsequious, almost fawning.

"My men and I are at your orders."

"I knew you would be cooperative," De Coursin replied with a hint of sarcasm that was lost on Aynard. "Perhaps your men could help us load the gold in our vehicles quickly."

"Certainly." Aynard gave orders for the loading.

De Coursin turned to Bastide. "Inspector Bastide?"

"Yes."

"The Minister is pleased with your work on this case."

"A lot of my men worked on it," Bastide replied. "Inspector Mattei particularly."

De Coursin smiled and nodded. "It won't be forgotten." He took Aynard by the arm. "Commissaire, I am leaving someone from the Ministry here to handle press queries about the case. I am also leaving a paper that will indicate how you are to handle the prisoners. They were misguided young men who had fallen under the spell of an old romantic. In fact, before he is brought to trial for the murders, it is very possible we will discover he is insane. As to the gold, there is adequate guidance in my instructions. Primarily, it consisted of a few old napoleons the colonel had collected. But there was never anything more. Understand?"

"I do."

"Now," De Coursin asked, "where is the Englishman? I'd like to talk to him—alone."

Bastide found Napier with Mattei in the back yard. He brought him to De Coursin. De Coursin waited till Bastide was out of earshot before he spoke.

"Good evening, Mr. Napier," De Coursin said in English. "You've had a difficult time."

"Bloody awful," Napier replied.

"I won't waste our time," De Coursin continued. "We're in the same business. I have a car waiting to take you to Marignane airport for a flight to London in one of our small jets. Under the circumstances, the sooner you get out of France the better."

Napier watched a policeman struggle by with a heavy sack. De Coursin grinned.

"Don't worry about the gold, *cher collègue*. We have been in touch with London. Our governments agree that the important thing is that no word of this be made public, now or in the future."

"I understand," Napier replied, rubbing his sore eyebrow.

"I'm not sure you do," De Coursin told him. "But even if I were not telling the truth, there is nothing you could do about it."

Napier shrugged. "I can't argue with that."

"This is Jacques," De Coursin said, introducing Napier to his assistant. "He will accompany you to the airport. *Bon voyage.*"

"I do have some things to fetch at the hotel and . . . at the Consulate."

"The hotel is no problem," De Coursin said, "but the Consulate . . . I would not recommend it. I am sure your people can handle that."

"Suppose you're right. Well, good-bye."

Jacques led Napier to the car. The Englishman turned and waved to Mattei. As he got into the sedan he asked Jacques if they might have a gin or two at the hotel.

"It's been a bit of an ordeal," he told the serious young Frenchman. "I feel the need of a slight pick-me-up."

Bastide watched a DGSE operative lead the colonel out the door. The old man stumbled on the steps and almost fell. The neighborhood lights came on again as the colonel approached Bastide. He seemed an emaciated corpse, his thin arms hanging slack at his sides. Bastide had seldom felt compassion for a murderer. For a few seconds he grieved for the man who used to be. The colonel banished that fleeting sympathy by spitting in Bastide's face.

It was a hot day. There wasn't a sign of a breeze. The fierce sun reflected from shop windows like static fire. Alley cats and neighborhood dogs lay in the shade ignoring each other. Passing cars left tire marks in the soft asphalt. Beyond the red-tiled roofs the surface of the Mediterranean sparkled blue and inviting.

The *patron* of the Café des Colonies wiped his face with a damp dishcloth. He turned to the door as Inspector Mattei pushed through the beaded curtain. Mattei was tired. He walked to the bar, noting he was the only customer, and nodded a greeting to the *patron*.

"*Alors?*" he said, "you wanted to talk to me?"

The *patron* poured a pastis, added ice water and pushed it across the bar.

"I'm glad you came early," the *patron* said, "before the others."

"Well?"

"It's about JoJo. Now that you have the people who killed the Englishman there should be no misunderstanding."

Mattei sipped the pastis, one eyebrow cocked. "Go on," he urged.

The *patron* put his beefy arms on the bar and leaned

toward Mattei. "There was no connection with JoJo's murder. It's a different story. Amer and his blacks. They did it."

"How do you know?"

"I know. I have good sources."

"Oh, there's no doubt of that. But something smells here. You've never volunteered anything before."

The *patron* pursed his lips. "This is different."

"How?"

"It's a question of honor."

"You're a born comic."

The *patron* looked hurt. "JoJo was a friend. We can't have outsiders coming in and stamping on us as if we were flies. This Amer doesn't belong in Marseille. He'll disrupt things."

"I can't go far on that," Mattei commented, finishing his pastis.

"And if we could deliver one of the killers?"

Mattei put both hands on the bar rail, nodding his head slowly. "That, I would consider. But I guarantee nothing."

"Don't underestimate us."

"Oh, I never have, believe me."

"Another pastis?"

"No. I have a family lunch waiting."

"Well, *bon appétit.*"

As Mattei walked out the door he saw Bouche d'Or approaching. He was dressed for the hot weather, with a battered panama on his head, an undershirt and dungaree trousers. He frowned when he saw Mattei and looked away quickly.

"*Bonjour, ami,*" Mattei greeted Bouche d'Or with exaggerated camaraderie. "I hope your girls are taking showers in this heat. If not, the vice squad can pick them up with their eyes closed."

"May your wife have twin pigs," the elderly pimp muttered as he entered the Café des Colonies.

Inspector Roger Bastide finished beating his *aïoli* sauce and tasted a fingerful from the wire whisk. It was perfect, golden and rich with egg yolks and garlic, smooth with quality olive oil. He added a bit more lemon juice, blended it in and put the bowl aside. The kitchen was hot and he was stripped to the waist. The fish for the *bourride* was done, firm and flaky. He'd found a fresh Mediterranean bass to add to the angler fish and hake. The broth was amber, redolent of thyme, fennel, bay leaf, tomatoes and saffron. He reduced the heat under the kettle and cut a dozen pieces of French bread from a crisp loaf. It would go into the bowl later to soak up the *bourride* when he was ready to serve. He glanced at his watch. It was almost one o'clock. Janine was late as usual. It didn't bother him. He'd learned to live with it.

He took a bottle of chilled, white Châteauneuf-du-Pape from the fridge and poured himself a glass. The coastal purists would say it didn't "marry well" with *bourride*. The hell with them. He liked its throat-warming body. He walked out onto the terrace and leaned on the railing. Even the yachts seemed to be moving slowly in the scorching sun, their sails flapping, sheets hanging slack. He felt the heat on his chest, closed his eyes and raised his face to the sun.

About the Author

Howard R. Simpson, a former U.S. Foreign Service officer, is now a consultant on international terrorism and a newspaper columnist. One of his last Foreign Service assignments was as American Consul General in Marseille in 1976. He is currently living in Europe. THE JUMPMASTER is his second novel for the Crime Club.